Anonymous

The Farmer and Planter

Vol. X No. 12

Anatiposi

Anonymous

The Farmer and Planter

Vol. X No. 12

Reprint of the original.

1st Edition 2023 | ISBN: 978-3-38230-608-3

Anatiposi Verlag is an imprint of Outlook Verlagsgesellschaft mbH.

Verlag (Publisher): Outlook Verlag GmbH, Zeilweg 44, 60439 Frankfurt, Deutschland
Vertretungsberechtigt (Authorized to represent): E. Roepke, Zeilweg 44, 60439 Frankfurt, Deutschland
Druck (Print): Books on Demand GmbH, In de Tarpen 42, 22848 Norderstedt, Deutschland

Vol. X., No. 12.   DECEMBER, 1859.   New Series, Vol. I., No. 12.

THE FARMER AND PLANTER

PRICE, $1 A YEAR, ALWAYS IN ADVANCE.

CONTENTS OF DECEMBER NUMBER.

AGRICULTURAL.

PAGE

Annual Address delivered before the "Darlington Agricultural Society," by E. E. EVANS.. 353
Guano, &c... 356
The Mole Track, The Subsoil Plow, and the Harrow.. 357
Philosophy of Rain.. 358
The Duration of Leaves.. 359
On Feeding of Stock.. 360
Brahmin Cattle.. 361
Sources of Fertility in soils..................................... 362
Balky Horses.. 363
Selection and Breeding of Sheep............................. 363
Midge, or Weevil... 364
Stock-Growing at the South...................................... 364
Cotton-Packing, and False Conjectures of the Crop.. 365
How to use Lime... 365
The Wheat Midge... 366
But one way to Farm.. 366
Sheep Husbandry in the West..................................... 366
Manner of Milking.. 367
Putting in Fall Wheat... 368
Sowing Wheat.. 368
Night Soil—Its Value... 368

EDITORIAL, COMMUNICATIONS, &c.

The end of Volume Ten—Our Future............................ 369
The Fair... 369
Nomenclature.. 369
Horses... 370
Brahmins... 370
Straw—Its Value as Food.. 370
Concentrated Manures.. 370
A South Carolina Mole-Track North of Mason and Dixon's Line.. 371
Country vs. City.. 371
The Guano Controversy... 371
Waste of Fertilizers... 372
Improved Farming.. 372

"Sanded Cotton."... 373
Horses.. 373
Hog Pens.. 374
The Fair.. 374
Fire-Proof Composition to Resist Fire for Five Hours... 375
Poultry... 375
To Keep Butter Hard and Cool.................................. 376
Comparative Values... 376
Receipts for Testing Eggs.. 376
Most Profitable Breed of Sheep................................. 376
Cure for Warts and Corns.. 376

HORTICULTURAL, POMOLOGICAL, &c.

Work for the Month.. 377
Susannah Apple... 377
Grapes for Florida.. 377
A large Lenoir Grape-Vine... 377
Two New Pears.. 378
Spanish Chesnuts, Madeira Nuts, &c.,.......................... 378
Country Life... 378
Who Bit Me... 379
The Apple-Tree Borer... 379
Management of Lawns.. 380
Salt Rising Bread... 381
Concrete Floors... 382
Keeping Grapes.. 382
Plants—Where they Originated.................................... 382
How a Chick is Hatched.. 383
Cleaning the Bark of Fruit-Trees............................... 383
A Plea for the Crow.. 383
The Elder Bush a Protection from Insects...................... 383
Hen Manure... 383

DOMESTIC ECONOMY, RECIPES, &c.

Saving Cabbage... 384
Labor-Saving Soap... 384
Clean Milking, &c., &c.,.. 384

SUBSCRIBE PROMPTLY.

We shall print an extra number of copies of our January issue, and if the patronage exceeds that edition we shall reprint it, but the March number will be limited to but a small amount beyond what is required for our subscription list, at that time, and unless the increase of subscribers will warrant us, we shall not reprint. We cannot afford to risk so great an outlay of paper, labor, and other materials, without a *reasonable* prospect of being sustained.

4000 SUBSCRIBERS

Is the smallest number that will ensure the continuance of the *Farmer and Planter* longer than next year; and that number must be secured by the time of our March issue, or it will be too late to secure copies. With the present patronage only, we intend to publish the 11th volume, equal in all respects to the past, although it yields not one dollar for the labors of Editors or Publisher. Shall it be sustained, or will the agriculturists of South Carolina kill off the last effort which, in all probability, will ever be made, to establish an agricultural journal in the State? We put this question, seriously, to every one of our subscribers, for we feel confident that, when this effort fails, no one will be found willing to risk time and money in a similar enterprise. It is now or never, for an agricultural journal in South Carolina.

VOL. X. DECEMBER, 1859. NO. 12.

R. M. STOKES, }
Proprietor }

COLUMBIA, S. C.

{ NEW SERIES
{ Vol. 1, No. 12.

From the Darlington Flag.

ANNUAL ADDRESS

Delivered before the " Darlington Agricultural Society," Sept. 8th, 1859, by Mr. Edward E. Evans.

The improvement of the agriculture of our own section, is the mission which we have assumed ; and it is a source of congratulation that the subject presents itself to us replete with encouragement. We have only to look back through a decade of years, to witness a condition of our agricultural interests to which the present affords a striking and gratifying contrast. Instead of a settled gloom, with regard to the price of our great staple, which then oppressed the Southern mind, and seemed to paralyze its energies, the future now promises so remunerating a return to the labors of the planter, as to bid fair to unsettle the rule of reason and launch us upon a period of reckless speculation. But it is to the improved condition of our soil itself to which I allude more particularly. But a few years back, and all over the face of our country might be seen deserted fields, surrendered to the sombre reign of the broomsedge and the pine, while he who had robbed the soil of its treasures, had abandoned it to hopeless sterility, and gone in search of a virgin soil. But to-day, a deserted field is scarcely to be found. An improved tillage has, more or less, restored what the ruthless hand of the former owner had destroyed, and where those funereal emblems of dead soil, the sedge and the pine, then held undisputed sway, the snowy fleece of our staple plant is just rewarding the ministering care of the planter, and that queen of cereals, our American corn, is waving in the breeze, as if exulting in the good mission for which it was designed by a merciful Providence. These, as isolated facts, are full of encouragement. But we are not to regard them as isolated facts. In these changes is involved a more pregnant meaning, which will appear upon reflection.

Man, in his connection with the soil, has always exhibited a two-fold character, as has been graphically illustrated by one of the first of modern agricultural chemists. We find him as the destroyer of the soil—he enters upon the forest, where nature has been for ages elaborating the elements of fertility ; he fells the trees ; he plows the soil. With a reckless system of culture he takes crop after crop, until exhausted nature will yield him no more. He then again enters upon the forest, where the same ruthless process is again performed. But to him succeeds another and better race. It is the renovator of the soil, whose mission it is to heal the wounds which the destroyer has inflicted. His march, though slow, is no less certain. Such has been the agricultural history of all countries. One race has exhausted the soil, another has restored. And the marked improvement in our own soil, to which I have alluded, is, to my mind, an evidence that the age of the destroyer is over, and that we are now upon the dawn of the better period of renovation.—Whatever may be the case elsewhere, with us, at least, I believe the soil has reached its lowest point of deterioration, and for the future, in the hands of a settled population whose minds are imbued with that noble sentiment, the love of home, it is destined to a steady, though it may be slow, improvement.

Now, what are the agencies which have led to our improved condition ? Upon a very slight reflection this must be ascribed to one prominent cause—a better knowledge and application of those material laws which govern our soils, and our plants, and the consequent introduction and general use of better methods of preparation, and in the manuring and cultivation of our crops. Now, with regard to the knowledge of those natural laws connected with our pursuit, it is evident that, while some progress has been made in breaking down grosser errors, and introducing better systems of planting, we are yet but upon the threshhold of improvement. When we look around us, we are at once struck with the variety and contradiction of systems and opinions which prevail. It might be supposed that every planter possessed a different soil, and that his crops obeyed different laws of life ; one plows deep, in preparing the soil for his seed—another shallow ; one advocates surface culture, and thinks the roots of the plants should not be injured ; another holds that the crop is greatly benefited by having its roots destroyed ; one puts his manure upon the surface— another contends that it cannot be placed sufficiently deep. In every operation there is confusion and contradiction. Now, whence this chaos of opinion ? Do the objects with which the planter deals constitute an exception to the general laws which govern other creations of Divine Power? Does a blind chance prevail, instead of a government of law ? Or has science ignored our pursuit ? While she has been lavish in shedding light upon those other arts which minister to the comfort of man, has she neglected this, upon which not only comfort but the very existence of life depends? Neither the one nor the other of these is correct. Fixed laws, founded in Divine wisdom, unerringly govern our soils, and direct the growth of our crops. Nor has science been idle in her efforts to advance this great pursuit of man. From the crude speculations of Jethro Tull, down to the more refined and certain researches of Liebig and Johnston, she has, at all times, been busy, either in grouping the individual phenomena of agriculture into laws and systems, or by careful analogies, reaching at one step at truths which individual experience might take years to accomplish ; and there is, to-day, as much true science connected with agriculture, as with any other of the practical arts of life. It is not so much to the want of knowledge, as the failure to apply it, that we must ascribe the unsettled condition of agricultural opinions. It becomes, Mr. President, a question of great practical value, to which I invite your attention : why our pursuit constitutes an exception among the arts of life, in rejecting the aid of science in ascertaining those laws which govern its operations ? This evil, I believe, has resulted simply from the failure in the general mind to recognise the true dignity of practical agriculture. The labors of the field, or the direct and personal management of the plantation, has not generally been thought an appropriate sphere for men of intellect and education ; its genial and invigorating labors have been neglected for the empty pursuit of public honors, or the over-crowded professions. To one who properly appreciates the true dignity of his avocation, the noble field of thought and research it affords, the sublime lessons of dependence and faith which it teaches, this erroneous opinion is calculated to excite not only astonishment, but indignation. But, however unaccountable this opinion, its effects have been, in the highest degree, pernicious. It has led to the separation of mind from labor—the divorcement of science from art—and, as a consequence, has led, in a great degree, to the formation of two distinct classes of agriculturists, both of which are wrong, and without a reunion of which no solid progress can be made —the theorist, and the so-called practical man.— Under this erroneous opinion, that there was nothing attractive or intellectual in the practical labors of the field, the man of education, to whom fortune had given agricultural property, has, in the main, given up its management to an agent, while he himself has embarked upon the demoralising career of political life, or to the barren pursuit of letters— or, where he has given his mind to the subject at all, he has been satisfied to acquire a knowledge of

theory in the closet. He masters the theory of soils and vegetable growth, but he does not go into the field, and at the foot of the plowshare acquire that practical knowledge which would enable him to turn theories to account. Of the daily routine of plantation life, he is utterly ignorant ; he can tell you why the soil should be deeply plowed, but, in the field, he cannot tell you when it is done, or whether the proper implement is employed. Such is the theoretical class of farmers. It is not strange, when, teeming with theory, they determine to unsettle the old order of things, and establish the reign of science, that it should result in utter failure. But the evil does not stop here ; this has a tendency to produce error equally great in the opposite direction. The great body of practical farmers of the country, men whom neither time nor education enable to investigate scientific truth, seeing the failure of this class, have come to conclude that any effort to apply science to agriculture is fraught with certain failure, and have come to believe that the only road to truth, in their pursuit, is by the tedious process of individual experience ; hence, they adhere tenaciously to those opinions based upon their own experience, or that of those just about them. Now, while I recognise experience as the only true basis of all knowledge, yet I believe there is no greater source of error than individual experiment, as ordinarily conducted ; opinion based upon this is usually the result of a single experiment, without taking into account the great variety of circumstances which not only modify, but may entirely distort the legitimate effects of any cause. Hence we find among the so-called practical men of the country, the most unreasonable and absurd opinions, based upon this spurious experience. Such are the two classes which we too frequently find—one possessing knowledge without practical skill, and the other skill without knowledge to guide them. Our agriculture will never occupy a healthy position, a position of progress, until these two classes shall have been combined ; until theoretical knowledge and practical skill shall meet in the same individual.

So long as the false opinions, of which I have spoken, shall separate intelligence from practical labor, the truths revealed by science must fail, from defective application, and be brought into disrepute among the great body of practical farmers. It is to the neglect to ascertain and apply those natural laws which govern our soils and our crops, and which science has, in a great measure revealed, that must be ascribed those crude and contradictory opinions to which I have alluded. It may be a labor of value to look into some of these opinions, and see if that scientific knowledge which has hitherto been neglected might not guide us to clearer views. Take that most important subject, the production and application of manures ; what crude and unsatisfactory opinions and pernicious treatment prevail here ! The chemist has long since, by analysis, revealed to us every element which constitutes our manures ; we know that these elements consist of two classes : the organic, which, whenever decomposition takes place, assume their gaseous form and pass into the atmosphere, and the inorganic, or mineral, which, when released by decomposition, being readily soluble in water, must, when exposed, be borne off by the rains; yet, notwithstanding this simple truth, what reckless treatment do we see every day in the management of manures! How often do we see herds of cattle folded for weeks upon open fields, while the scorching sun and bleaching rains are busy in the work of destruction, and because this ruthless treatment does not entirely destroy the value of the manure, it is contended that this is the most economical mode of manuring with our stock. And so, too, with our cotton seed, that richest and most volatile of all vegetable substances. The planter seems perfectly satisfied if his heap of seed does not diminish too much in bulk, while the atmosphere, loaded with its pungent odors, should admonish him that he is losing that very element, which, by a heavy outlay in guano, he seeks to furnish to his crops. And here I would allude to another error prevailing among the more enterprising class of planters; this class, seeing the necessity of furnishing to the exhausted soil a larger supply of food for their crops, have sought to increase rather the quantity than the quality of their manures, and for this purpose they advocate keeping larger stocks of cattle. Now, I contend that there can be no greater absurdity than feeding, or keeping upon our uncultivated fields, which is the same in effect, stocks of cattle, for the *mere* purpose of making manure; I say *mere* purpose, because, where the stock itself is a source of income, as in England and the continental States of Europe, and in portions of our own country, it presents a different question; there this system prevails, and is merely one of mixed husbandry. What is the manure of the animal but the food which it has consumed, with the loss of that portion which has gone to keep up the vitality of the animal; the animal itself can add nothing to it—the manure is more immediately active than the food of which it is the mere *debris*, because it is at once placed in a fermented state, and for the further reason that the nitrogenous element has become relatively, but only relatively, increased. There does not exist in the manure a single element, or portion of element, which did not exist in the food. It is a fact of universal experience, that the value of the manure depends entirely upon the food upon which the animal has been fed; where valuable pastures are adjacent to the fields, then, but in no other case, may we employ large herds of cattle to transfer the vegetation of the pasture to our compost heaps. I believe, Mr. President, that we must look rather to an increased efficiency of our animal manure, than to an increase of its quantity, by preserving and composting upon correct principles, the manure of those necessary animals, which we are compelled to keep on the plantation. And so, too, in the application of manures, the same confusion and contradiction exists. One contends that it should always be placed and kept upon the surface; another, that it can never be too deeply buried. Now, it seems to me that a simple knowledge of the substances which compose our manures, and the losses to which they are liable; would at all times furnish us with a sure guide to their application. Where the manure is chiefly valuable for its organic elements, such as cotton-seed and all animal manures, including guano, a simple deduction should teach us that it cannot be too thoroughly buried, or incorporated with the soil, provided it be not placed beyond atmospheric action; and, on the other hand, where our manures are inorganic or mineral, such as salt, and lime in all its forms, it should by all means be placed on the surface. And yet it is the general practice of the country to put cotton-seed on the surface, *around* the corn, and I have known the super-phosphate of lime buried as deeply and carefully under the bed, as if there was danger of its exploding in a gaseous form.

And look at another subject of plantation economy of scarcely minor importance to manuring. The great desideratum on our thin soils, is, to make the plantation self-sustaining in food. While our cotton crops are far from abundant, a considerable portion of the income of the country is expended in the purchase of grain. It would seem that if science could throw any light upon the subject, it would be eagerly and earnestly sought after. There can be no doubt but that the ordinary mode of feeding our grain in an uncrushed state, is in direct conflict with well-established truths. Science tells us, that, for the purpose of preserving its vital principle, nature has enveloped all grain in a coating, or husk, which almost defies the action of gastric juice. For this reason, when the food reaches the stomach imperfectly masticated, it must, to a great extent, pass through the system undigested, and thus, to all purposes, be lost to the animal. The amount of grain thus wasted, must have arrested the attention of every one, and its cause just stated, should teach us the importance of using ground food, instead of the present wasteful system. An experience of several years has satisfied me, that, with an amount of labor scarcely worthy of mention, in the use of an ordinary cob-mill, an annual saving of at least one-fourth may be made on the plantation; we thus not only place the grain in the best condition for digestion, but we get the benefit of the nutritious element of the cob. But, in reply to this, we are told, that nature has furnished our animals with organs for this very function, and it is therefore a work of idle supererogation to assist them; forgetting that man, who is similarly endowed, not only grinds his food, but employs all the art of the *cuisine* to assist his digestion.

Another illustration of how little opinions are based on correct knowledge, may be found in the ready susceptibility of the agricultural mind to imposition. It is a constantly recurring fact, that some new agricultural product is announced to the world, which, without regard to soil or cultivation, is to yield marvelous crops. Now, a just knowledge upon this subject would teach us that one plant can excel another of the same species, only in a greater tendency to make fruit; the plant, as such, can make nothing, and unless the elements of fertility exist in the soil, either from nature or art, that very tendency to fruitfulness is itself the source of failure. But nothing has ever yet been presented with pretensions so extravagant as not to meet with ready credulity; everything has been received, imperfectly tested, and, because it did not meet expectations founded only in ignorance, has been summarily condemned. Such has been the fate of many improved varieties of our staple plants. Such, for example, as the

Peabody corn, a variety of our common corn, in which the fruiting tendency has, by selection, been highly developed, and which, under high manuring and culture, may, in favorable seasons, be made to produce enormous crops; but for ordinary, unmanured soils, and indifferent culture, it is, necessarily, one of the poorest of all varieties. So, too, of that wonderful plant, the Chinese millet; we remember the enthusiasm which greeted its advent, while to-day there is scarcely one to do it reverence. There can be no doubt of the great value of this plant. As a soiling crop for hogs, in which I have tested it fully, it has no rival, yielding, as it does, four-fold more of healthy and nutritious food than any other known plant. But while conceding its value, it has generally been condemned because it was too great an exhauster; as if any plant could be of value, which did not exhaust the soil! What is it to exhaust the soil, but to convert its dead elements into living food for man? That plant is of most value which exhausts most, provided it produces food of value. Such an anomaly as a plant affording nutritious food, and, at the same time, not exhausting the soil, has never been known.

I have thus glanced at some few of the better class of these practical errors, as illustrations of my position—that the practical agriculture of the country is immeasurably below those truths which science has revealed. I have ascribed this to the fact that, from a false estimate of our pursuit, the educated men of the country, whose minds are open to scientific truths, have not, by devoting themselves practically to agriculture, acquired that skill which would enable them successfully to apply those truths, and thus commend them to general adoption. But it is one of the auspicious omens of the future, that the true intellectual status of our pursuit is beginning to be recognised. We see it in the establishment of agricultural societies, in the diffusion of agricultural literature, in the demand for agricultural schools—and we see it here, to-day, in this assemblage of intelligent planters—an evidence that here, at least, our cherished vocation is destined to command, not only the best industry, but the best mind of the country. I trust that this is to be a growing feeling, until the general sentiment of the country shall be that of the great Diocletian, who found the humble labors of the garden more congenial than the cares of state, and "took more pleasure in the cultivation of a few pot herbs, than in all the honors which the empire had ever conferred." And when we shall have realized this state of public sentiment, and not till then, will our agriculture emerge from its present crude and fragmentary condition, into a perfect system, built in fair proportion upon the well ascertained and recognised laws of nature.

For the Farmer and Planter.
GUANO, &c.

Mr. Editor:—Several communications having lately appeared in your valuable paper in reference to the "Guano Dynasty"—some praising and some censuring—I desire to give my humble experience in the matter, in a style that I hope will be both "short and sweet." In the first place, I believe the guano fever to be like most malignant maladies, *contagious*, and when once contracted, requires considerable purging. Start a flock of sheep down a steep hill, and if nineteen out of twenty break their necks, the twentieth one will do the same, in order to follow suit. It is the same with dogs.— If you start a single dog to barking in Carolina, if convenient hearing distances could be afforded, through the entire distance, the last howl would be heard in the State of Maine. I have seen my old friend, Josh C——, start every dog in Columbia to barking, by the gratification of his own canine propensities. I fear it is too much the case with human nature, and while I make the sweeping charge, I include myself; but having been humbugged several times, during a life-time of twenty-five years, I have commenced, at last, to do *my own thinking*, and what suggestions I make are reaped from the school of experience.

I do not think, Mr. Editor, that guano is what it has been "cracked up" to be. I, for one, have smelt treason (or something else of the kind,) in the tainted gale, and am ready to sound the cry of alarm, and though I have no idea of being half so fortunate as the goose that saved the city of Rome, I cannot but think that a little common sense, by the way of practical experience, might do some little good.

Last January I bought five tons of guano, in the city of Charleston, and having been selected by a gentleman of character and experience, it proved to be a number one article. It cost me $70 per ton, to have it landed at the nearest depot, making the cost of the five tons $350, commissions $8.75, interest on cost, until sale of present crop, $24.50, cost of hauling, $10. Nothing for application. The total cost, then, will be $393.25. I applied this guano to my whole crop, consisting of twenty-four acres of cotton, and one hundred and thirty acres of corn. I made eight bales of cotton, and one thousand bushels of corn, shucked, shelled and measured. The cotton, at the rate of $40 per bale, will amount to $432 nett, and the corn to $1,000, making $1,432 for my crop. The smallest crop that ever has been made on the same land was five bales of cotton, and seven hundred and eighty bushels of corn, making, at the same ratio, $980. To this add the cost of the guano, $393.25, and the nett profit of my guano will be $58.75, on an outlay of $400, which amount will be more than eat up by increased trouble. The land that I planted was all rested for the last year, and a small portion for two years.— Would not the profit be less on lands that are constantly planted? I think it would. I don't expect to buy any more guano, unless it falls to $40 or $50 per ton. It may pay at these rates. I had good teams, plows and hands, and a "crack Overseer."

The truth of the matter is, Mr. Editor, that highly concentrated manures, at exorbitant prices, is not the proper policy for the planters of South Carolina to pursue. We will have to return to the piney woods, and rake straw as our parents did—not because daddy did it, but because common sense teaches us that it is right. The first thing necessary is to keep the fire off our lands. There is a great propensity down here, in the backwoods, to set fire to the woods every Spring, for the benefit of the *keows*, and mostly, too, by men who never had a *keow*. I, for one, will never suffer fire on my land, and if the same policy was universally pursued, there would never be any difficulty in making enough manure, on idle occasions, to keep us busy the whole Spring in applying to our lands.

I have had considerable difficulty, nay, impossibility, in convincing the people, where I live, that burning land is an injury to the land itself, independent of the total destruction of compost manure. They contend that the land is the *essential* in making a crop. I contend that flour makes very good bread, but much better with salt and lard.

Upon the whole, Mr. Editor, I think that in proper drainage, deep plowing, and a liberal application of compost manures, we have, within ourselves, all the appliances necessary to good crops. With these we can make as much as we can gather, and that is enough to satisfy a reasonable mind.

Very respectfully,

CYPRESS FORK.

Marion, S. C., Oct. 15th, 1859.

From the Working Farmer.

THE MOLE TRACK, THE SUBSOIL PLOW, AND THE HARROW.

Who has not observed the pulverulent condition of the soil immediately over the mole-track? This little animal travels beneath the surface, and all the soil above him is rendered finer, that is, more divided, than by a thousand plowings. What does he do to it, and how?

Is it necessary to disintegrate soil, that masses should be moved through the arc of a circle of twenty-three inches diameter, and placed in a new locality? Or, is it only necessary that each particle of soil should be moved relatively to those which surround it the millionth of an inch? We claim the latter, and that the mole-track performs this.

Such were our observations many years ago, and we tried to induce the plow-makers to make steel mole, which, by mechanical force, should be propelled through the ground, imitating the effect of this little animal, and rendering the soil above its track a hundred times better conditioned than any mould-board plow could leave it. This was indeed a difficult task; we showed it to all the large manufacturers, and did not succeed in inducing them to undertake it; at last Mr. Nourse, of the firm of Nourse, Mason & Co., of Boston, agreed to make the experiment. He did so, in part, by building what is known as the reversible lifting subsoil plow. This acted so much better than the old-style subsoil plow, with the wing at its side, that it induced a nearer proximation to our views in the building of what is now know as the lifting-subsoil plow, made of steel, and representing on its upper side an arrow-head, or spear-head, laying flat, with its under side hollowed out ; this, in its horizontal position, is connected with the plow-beam above by a scimetar knife in front and an angular supporter in its rear; the resolution of the force of the horse is received upon the point, and divided through these upright supports and the beam, and perfectly expended in the direction of their length, and not in that of their horizontal cut section. The forcing forward through the soil parallel to the surface, and nineteen inches below it, of this compressed V, or wedge of steel, imitates the travel of the mole; and, strange to say, all the soil above it is separated, particle from particle—all the tendencies of the inclined plane or planes on the surface of this wedge of steel being upward and outward. The disintegration is not confined to the width of the wedge traveling below and imitating the mole, but every particle of soil between its line of travel and the surface, is slightly separated from its fellow, leaving all, except the upper inch, which has nothing but the atmosphere to impinge against, as finely divided as if sieved, and to a width of twenty-four inches at the surface of the ground. It is for this reason that the running of a subsoil plow through an old and partly exhausted meadow, loosens the soil to the full depth of seventeen, eighteen, or nineteen inches, leaving the surface-sod softened, and admitting the atmosphere for the rejuvenation of the soil. The old roots, by atmospheric influence, decay, the new establish themselves, and by moderate top-dressings the old pasture is restored, and may again be mowed, without first taking it out of grass and carrying it through a rotation of crops.

The day will yet arrive when every implement intended for the disintegration of the soil will embrace this principle. It surpasses all the mammoth schemes of plowing by steam, with the ordinary surface-plow; it appeals to natural law, in its easiest and most natural form; it is indicated by the ground-mole, and the hints thrown out in nature's simplest economy, are always the guideboards to success. Every fish preceded the calculations of mathematicians in defining the form of least resistance; the bee forestalled the architect in building the roof to each cell of the honey-comb composed of three planes ; the power of the bird to convex his eye so as to observe the animalcule, and feed upon it, and flatten his eye so as to observe his enemy, the hawk, at a distance, anticipated all that every optician has since rendered valuable ; and the telescope is but an appropriation, in a mechanical form, of the functions of the bird's eye. So is it with a despised mole; he will yet teach man the true mode of disintegrating the soil. We have a small steel mole attached to a beam, which we call a one-horse lifting-subsoil plow, which, on our farm, does the work of forty men with digging forks or spades. When corn is one inch high, or such row crops as beets, carrots, parsnips, turnips, etc., are just peeping above the ground, this implement can be run between the rows so as to lift them in common with the soil they inhabit, for so slight a distance, as not to abrade the roots, but simply to loosen the soil in the relation of the particles to each other, permitting the roots to extend themselves, and leaving the soil, even after the crop has appeared beyond the surface of the ground, in a finer tilth, to a depth of twelve inches, than could be obtained by a hundred surface plowings. Thus the new roots may travel to a depth where drought is unknown—where the temperature of the soil is $1\frac{1}{2}°$, or more, colder than the supernatant atmosphere, and where the chemistry of nature is actively progressive, yielding up the riches of the soil to the freshly condensed humidity of the atmosphere, ladened with such gasses as are consequent upon organic decomposition, and assists the humidity to dissolve the inorganic food required by the crop. Such a steel mole does the work with us of forty men, and such may be seen at our office, by those who choose to examine it.

A larger implement of this kind, suited to two horses, and capable of traveling at a depth of nineteen inches, is a proper subsoil plow, and entirely superior to the old style implement now on sale, we are sorry to say, at many of the agricultural warehouses. This new implement may be run by a separate team following the surface-plow, with its beam lying in the bottom of the surface-plow's furrow, and disintegrating the subsoil, without elevating it, to a depth of nineteen inches below the surface-plowing. Suppose, then, the surface-plowing to be ten inches, we have a total depth disintegrated of twenty-nine inches, into which atmosphere and roots may both travel, and thus, the character of the subsoil will rapidly change to that of the surface. Each year the farmer may deepen his surface-soil plowing an inch or more, and he will soon discover that his more valuable farm is beneath that which he formerly cultivated. Less manure will produce a larger amount of crops; he defies drought; and he has not the trouble of moving West to look for new land, if he spends the same amount to furnish judicious fertilizers, which would be required to pay the cartage on barn-yard manures given him, at half a mile from his gate; he will beat the results of any old-style farmer, who appeals to barn-yard manure alone, and who asks himself "how little manure will answer to raise a crop, instead of ascertaining how much manure he may use with increased profit."

This larger sub-soil plow should be propelled by oxen, for then a chain may be used, permitting the beam to descend to the bottom of the surface-plow's furrow, whereas, when horses are used with a whiffletree, the whiffletree rests upon the furrow-surface, and prevents the descent of the sub-soil plow beam. We would not accept the best farm in America, and agree to cultivate it as a business, if debarred from the use of the lifting-sub-soil plow, both in preparing the land, and in the after cultivation of the crops with one of a smaller size.

Those of our readers who wish to see its operation, may do so at our farm, where they will always find a team and a sub-soil plow ready to be exhibited to them, and subject to their control and experiment.

How different is this operation, both in principle and effect, from the common harrow, and all other analogous implements. This is a succession of cones, point downward, which is continually compacting the soil, raising the harrow, by its newly acquired stubbornness, and, in turn, compacting the next inch above, until, by its continued use, the ground may be rendered as hard as if rammed by a pile driver, so that it cannot even be plowed. With this truth before us, why will farmers use the harrow, under the delusion that it is a disintegrating implement? It should never be used, except in the lightest form, to rake weeds off of surfaces, previously fully prepared and in the lightest tilth; for every lump the harrow breaks, it compacts finer soil below it. We hope its days are numbered, and but few.

PHILOSOPHY OF RAIN.

To understand the philosophy of this beautiful and often sublime phenomena, so often witnessed since the creation of the world, and essential to the very existence of animals, a few facts derived from observation and a long train of experiments must be remembered:

1. Were the atmosphere, everywhere, at all times, at a uniform temperature, we should never have rain, or hail, or snow. The water absorbed by it in evaporation from the sea and the earth's surface, would descend in an imperceptible vapor, or cease to be absorbed by the air when once fully saturated.

2. The absorbing power of the atmosphere, and consequently its capability to retain humidity, is proportionally greater in warm than in cold air.

3. The air near the surface of the earth is warmer than it is in the region of the clouds. The higher we ascend from earth, the colder do we find the atmosphere. Hence the perpetual snow on very high mountains in the hottest climates. Now, when from continual evaporation the air is highly saturated with vapor, though it be invisible and the sky cloudless, if its temperature is suddenly reduced by cold currents descending from above, or rushing from a higher to a lower latitude, its capacity to retain moisture is diminished, clouds are formed, and the result is rain. Air condenses as it cools, and like a sponge filled with water and compressed, pours out the water which its diminished capacity cannot hold. How singular yet how simple the philosophy of rain!— What but Omniscience could have devised such an admirable arrangement for watering the earth?—*Scientific Journal.*

Farmers should remember that a tubful of soap-suds is worth as much as a wheel-barrow of good manure. Every bucket of soap-suds should be thrown where it will not be lost. The garden is a good and convenient place to dispose of it; but the roots of grape-vines, young trees, or anything of that sort, will do as well.

From Life Illustrated.

THE DURATION OF LEAVES.

Leaves last only for a limited period, and are thrown off, or else perish or decay on the stem, after having fulfilled their office for a certain time.— In view of their duration, leaves are called *fugacious*, when they fall off soon after their appearance, *deciduous*, when they last only for a single season, and *persistent*, when they remain through the cold season, or other interval during which vegetation is interrupted, and until after the appearance of new leaves, so that the stem is never leafless, as in *Evergreens*.

Leaves last only for a single year in many Evergreens, as well as in desiduous-leaved plants; the old leaves falling soon after those of the ensuing season are expanded; or, if they remain longer, ceasing to bear any active part in the economy of the vegetable, and soon losing their vitality altogether. In pines and firs, however, although there is annual fall of leaves either in autumn or spring, yet these were the produce of some season earlier than the last; and the branches are continually clothed with foliage of from two to five, or even eight or ten successive years. On the other hand, it is seldom that all the leaves of an herb endure through the whole growing season, the earlier foliage near the base of the stem perishing while fresh leaves are still appearing above. In our deciduous trees and shrubs, however, the leaves of the season are mostly developed within a short period, and they all perish nearly at the same time. They are not destroyed by frost, as is commonly supposed; for they begin to languish, and often assume their autumnal tints, (as happens with the red maple especially,) or even fall, before the earlier frosts; and when vernal vegetation is destroyed by frost, the leaves blacken and wither, but do not fall off entire, as they do in autumn. Some leaves are cast off, indeed, while their tissues have by no means lost their vitality. Death is often rather a consequence than the cause of the fall. Others die and decay on the stem without falling, as in Palms and most Endogens. In some cases many of the dead leaves hang on the branches through the winter, as in the Beech, falling only when the new buds expand the following spring.—

We must therefore, distinguish between the death and the fall of the leaf.

THE FALL OF THE LEAF.

Is owing to an organic separation, through an *articulation*, or joint, which forms between the base of the petiole, (leaf stalk,) and the surface of the stem on which it rests. The formation of the articulation is a vital process, a kind of disintegration of a transverse layer of cells, which cuts off the petiole by a regular line, in a perfectly uniform manner in each species, leaving a clean scar at the insertion. The solution of continuity begins in the epidermis, (the skin of the plant,) where a faint line marks the position of the future joint, while the leaf is still young and vigorous; later, the line of demarkation becomes well marked, internally as well as externally; the disintegrating process advances from without inwards, until it reaches the woody bundles, and the side next the stem, which is to form the surface of the scar, has a layer of cells condensed into what appears like a prolongation of the epidermis, so that, when the leaf separates, "the tree does not suffer from the effects of an open wound." "The provision for the separation being once complete, it requires little to effect it; a desiccation of one side of the leaf stalk, by causing an effort of tortion, will readily break through the small remains of the fibro-vascular bundles, or the increased size of the coming leaf-bud will snap them; or, if these causes are not in operation, a gust of wind, a heavy shower, or even the simple weight of the lamina will be enough to disrupt the small connections, and send the suicidal member to its grave. Such is the history of the fall of the leaf. We have found that it is not an accidental occurrence, arising simply from the vicissitudes of temperature and the like, but a regular and vital process, which commences with the first formation of the organ, and is completed only when that is no longer useful; and we cannot help admiring the wonderful provision that heals the wound, even before it is absolutely made, and affords a covering from atmospheric changes, before the part can be subjected to them."[*] Leaves fall by an articulation, in most Oxygenous plants, where the insertion usually occupies only a moderate part of the circumference of the stem, and especially in those with woody stems which continue to increase in diameter. When they are not cast off in autumn, therefore, the disruption inevitably takes place the next spring, or whenever the circumference further enlarges. But in most Endogenous plants, where the leaves are scarcely, if at all, articulated with the stem, which increases little in diameter, subsequent to its early growth, they are not thrown off, but simply wither and decay; their dead bases, or petioles, being often persistent for a long time.

THE DEATH OF THE LEAF,

However, in these and other cases, is still to be explained. Why have leaves such a temporary existence? Why, in ordinary cases, do they last only for a single year, or a single summer? An answer to this question is to be found in the anatomical structure of the leaf, and the nature and amount of the fluid which it receives and exhales. The water continually absorbed by the roots dissolves, as it percolates the soil, a small portion of earthy matter.— In limestone districts, especially, it takes up a sensible quantity of carbonate and sulphate of lime, and becomes *hard*. It likewise dissolves a smaller proportion of silex, magnesia, potash, etc. A part of this mineral matter is at once deposited in the woody tissue of the stem, but a larger portion is carried into the leaves, where, as the water is exhaled pure, all this earthy substance, not being volatile, must be left behind to incrust the delicate cells of the parenchyma, much as the vessels in which water is boiled for culinary purposes are in time incrusted with an earthy deposit. This earthy incrustation, in connection with the deposition of organic solidified matter, must gradually choke the tissue of the leaf, and finally unfit it for the performance of its

* Dr. Inman, in Henfrey's *Botanical Gazette*, vol. 1, page 61.

offices. Hence the fresh leaves most actively fulfil their functions in spring and early summer, but languish toward autumn, and ere long inevitably perish. Hence, although the roots and branches may be permanent, the necessity that the leaves should be annually renewed. But the former are in fact, annually renewed likewise; and life abandons the annual layers of wood and bark almost as soon as it does the leaves they supply, and for similar reasons; although their situation is such that they become part of a permanent structure, and serve to convey the sap, even when no longer endowed with vitality.

The general correctness of this view may be tested by direct microscopical observation. That this deposit consists in great part of earthy matter, is shown by carefully burning away the organic materials of an autumnal leaf over a lamp, and examining the ashes by a microscope, which will be found very perfectly to exhibit the form of the cells. The ashes which remain when a leaf or other vegetable substance is burned in the open air, represent the earthy materials which it has accumulated. A vernal leaf leaves only a small quantity of ashes; an autumnal leaf yields a very large proportion—from ten to thirty times as much as the wood from the same species, although the leaves contain the deposit of a single season only, while the heart-wood is loaded with the accumulations of successive years.

The dried leaves of the Elm contain more than eleven per cent. of ashes, while the wood contains less than two per cent.; those of the Willow more than eight per cent, while the wood has only 0.45; those of the Beech, 6.69, the wood only 0.36; those of the (European) Oak, 4.05, the wood only 0.21; those of the Pitch-Pine, 3.15, the wood only 0.25 per cent. Hence the decaying foliage in our forests restores to the soil a large proportion of the inorganic matter which the trees from year to year take from it.

ON THE FEEDING OF STOCK.

The feeding of stock is exactly one of those subjects which can be most successfully advanced by studying the principles on which it depends; and though these involve many most complex, chemical and physiological questions, we have obtained some foundation on which to go. The food which an animal consumes is partly assimilated and partly excreted, but, if it be properly proportioned to its requirements, its weight remains constant, and hence we learn that food does not remain permanently in the body. If, now, an animal be deprived of food, it loses weight, owing to the substances stored up in the body being used to maintain the process of respiration and the waste of the tissues. The course of events within the body is, so far as known, somewhat of this kind: The food is digested, absorbed into the blood, a certain quantity being consumed to support respiration. If the food be properly adjusted to the requirements of the animal, its weight remains unchanged—the quantity absorbed, and that excreted, exactly correspond to one another; but, if we increase the food, a part of the excess will be deposited in the tissues, to add to its weight. Now, the quantity absorbed depends upon the state

of the animal—a lean beast thoroughly exhausting its food, while, when it is nearly fat, it takes only a small proportion. So, likewise, if the quantity of food be greater than the digestive organs can well dispose of, a certain quantity escapes digestion altogether, and is practically lost.

The problem which the feeder has to solve is, how to supply his cattle with such food, and in such proportions, as to ensure the largest increase with the smallest loss. In solving this problem we must, in the first place, consider the general nature of the food of all animals, the constituents of which may be divided into three great classes—the nitrogenous matters, which go to the formation of flesh; the saccharine and oily, which support respiration and form fat. It is sufficiently obvious that, as the two great functions of nutrition and respiration must proceed simultaneously, the most advantageous food will be that which supplies them in the most readily assimilated forms, and in proper proportions. In regard to the first of these matters, it will be obvious, that, if two foods contain the same quantity of nutritive matters, but in one they are associated with a larger quantity of woody fibre or other non-nutritious matter, the latter will have considerably less value than the former.

The necessity for a proper balance of the two great classes of nutritive constituents, is also sufficiently obvious; for if, for example, an animal be supplied with a large quantity of nitrogenous matters, and a small amount of respiratory elements, it must, to supply a sufficiency of the latter, consume a much larger quantity of the former than it can assimilate, and there is practically a great loss. We may determine the proper proportion of these substances in three different ways: 1st, we may determine the composition of the animal body; 2d, we may examine that of the milk, the typical food of the young animal; and 3d, the results of actual feeding experiments may be examined.— But, however valuable the data derived from these experiments may be, they are less important than those derived from actual feeding experiments. In fact, it by no means follows, that the proportions in which the different substances are found in the animal are exactly those in which they ought to exist in the food. On the contrary, it appears that while one-tenth of the saccharine and faulty matters are assimilated by the animals, only one-twentieth of the nitrogenous compounds, and one-thirty-third of the mineral substances in the food, are assimilated by the animal. On the other hand, however, it must be remembered that the particular compounds also exercise a very different influence. Thus, a pound of fat in the food, when assimilated, will produce a pound of fat in the animal; but it requires about two-and-a-half pounds of sugar and starch to produce the same effect.

The broad, general principle arrived at is, that we must afford a sufficient supply of readily assimilable food, containing a proper proportion of each class of nutritive substances. But there are other matters to be borne in mind, for the food must not only increase the weight of the animal, but also support respiration and animal heat; and the quantity of food required for this purpose is large. It appears, from Boussingault's experiments, that, in a cow, eighteen ounces of nitrogenous matter are required to counterbalance the waste of the tissues—a quantity contained in about ten or twelve pounds of wheat flour—and it is well known that an ox expires four or five pounds of carbon daily, to supply which one hundred pounds of turnips are required. We see from this the large quantity, relatively to that used up, which is required for the maintenance of these functions, and the importance of adopting such measures as, by restraining them within the narrowest possible limits, produce a saving of food. The diminution of muscular exertion, and keeping the animals warm, so that a small quantity of food may be required to act as fuel to maintain the animal heat, are the most important considerations.— Although the presence of a sufficient quantity of nutritive matters is an essential qualification of all foods, their mechanical condition is not unimportant, for unless its bulk be such as to admit of the stomach acting upon it properly, there must be an appreciable loss; and there is no greater fallacy than to suppose that the best results are to be obtained by the use of those which contain their nutritive matters in a very small bulk.

As a practical question, the principles of feeding are restricted to determining how the staple food produced on the farm can be most advantageously used to feed the cattle kept on it, and on this point much requires to be said. It appears that they can be best made use of when combined with more highly nutritious food, such as oil-cake or rape; and, when this is properly done, a very great advantage is derived. It appears, from experiments, that sheep which, when fed on hay only, attain a weight of ninety pounds, reach a hundred when rape is added. *From a Lecture by* Dr. ANDERSON, *at the Highland (Scotland) Society's Show.*

From the American Stock Journal.

BRAHMIN CATTLE.

The Zebu differs greatly in size in different parts of Hindostan, and other countries of the East.— Like many species, he dwindles towards the countries of the Pacific, so that, in Corea, and the Islands of Japan he is little larger than a hog, showing that these countries are at the limits of the natural habitat of the species. The finest breeds of the Eastern Zebu are produced in the northern provinces of India. There they are tall and graceful animals, surpassing in the power of active motion any of the races of oxen with which we are conversant in Europe. They are used for the saddle, for chariots, for the bearing of burdens, for common draft, and all the labors of the field. They accompany the predatory armies of Indian nations in thousands, carrying materials of war. They are used in state processions by the princes of India. They are guided by a cord passed through the septum of the nose, to which are attached the bridle-reins, which, when not used, rest upon the hump of the shoulder. Their motion is easy, and they trot and gallop almost as freely as a horse. They have great powers of endurance, frequently traveling sixty or eighty miles a-day. When employed in chariots or the plough, they draw by a yoke, which rests upon the shoulder. They are exceedingly tractable, and be-

NEW SERIES, VOL. 1,—46.

come attached to their keepers. The milk-white color is esteemed by the Hindoos, which it likewise was by the ancient Egyptians, as having a character of sanctity. Very often rich Hindoos dedicate a particular bull of the sacred color to Siva, when he is branded by the emblem of the god, and thenceforward becomes exempt from the contumely of servitude. He wanders where he will, and no one strikes, molests, or turns him from his path; he feeds in the gardens, the rice fields, or wherever he chooses to enter; he finds his way into the market-places of towns and helps himself to the green herbs and choicest fruits, without any one driving him away. Impunity renders him familiar; he will take food from the hand like a dog, and everywhere dainties are presented to him by simple devotees. These consecrated bulls are described by English residents as absolute pests in the villages of India, thrusting their noses into the stalls of fruiterers and pastry-cooks, robbing the peasants of their little treasure, and helping themselves to whatever they please.— The reverence, however, paid to the bull and the cow is not extended to the emasculated Ox, who is treated with the utmost harshness, under the solitary exception of obedience to the law common to the Hindoos and Jews, of not muzzling the ox, when he treadeth out the corn.

Examples of the larger, as well as smaller races of these animals have been frequently brought to England, and they have been made to cross with the common breeds of the country. The mixed offspring are fruitful with one another, and the characteristic hump disappears with the first cross. In the year 1832, a bull and cow, of the finer breed, were exhibited at the Christmas Smithfield Show in London, under the name of Nagpore cattle. The following account of them, derived from Mr. Perkins, to whom they belonged, is given by Mr. Youatt, in his valuable Treatise on cattle, contained in the Library of Useful Knowledge.

"They were bred by Lieutenant-Colonel Skinner, at his farm at Danah, near Pokah, on the borders of the Bichaneer desert, 100 miles to the westward of Delhi. They are not Buffaloes, but of the highest breed of Indian cattle. They are used in India by the higher orders to draw their state carriages, and are much valued for their size, speed, and endurance, and sell at very high prices. These specimens arrived at Calcutta, a distance of 1400 miles, in January, 1829, and were then something under six months old. They were sent as a present to Mr. Wood, who was then residing at Calcutta, and by whom they were presented to Mr. Perkins. Col. Skinner has a large stock of them, and six or seven beasts are always kept saddled to carry the military dispatches. They remain saddled three or four hours, and, if not wanted in that time, fresh ones are brought to relieve their companions. They will travel with a soldier on their back fifteen or sixteen hours a-day, at the rate of six miles an hour. Their action is particularly fine. nothing like that of the English cattle, with the sideway circular action of their hind-legs; the Nagpore cattle bring their hind-legs under them in as straight a line as the horse. They are very active, and can clear a five-barred gate with the greatest ease. Mr. Perkins has a calf which has leaped over an iron fence higher than any five-barred gate ; and the bull frequently jumps over the same fence, in order to get at the water, and, when he has drunk his fill, leaps back again. The bull was in high condition when exhibited.— He is employed in a light cart in various jobs about the farm. Sometimes he goes fore-horse in the wagon-team to deliver corn ; he also drags the bush-harrow, and draws the light roller over the ploughed land. He is very docile and tractable when one man drives him and attends upon him, but he has now and then shown symptoms of dislike to others. He is fed entirely on hay, except that, when he works, a little bran is given to him, and, in the turnip season, he is treated occasionally with a few slices of Swedes, of which he is very fond. He was at first very troublesome to shoe, and it was necessary to erect a break in order to confine him. He was unwilling to go into it for some time, but now walks in it very contentedly. He is very fond of being noticed ; and often, when he is lying down, if any one, to whom he is accustomed, goes and sits down upon him and strokes him over the face, he will turn round and put his head on their lap, and lie there contentedly as long as they please. The cow is at grass with the milch cows, and comes up with them morning and evening when they are driven to be milked."

From the Boston Cultivator.

SOURCES OF FERTILITY IN SOILS.

Liebig, in his chemical researches, says : "If we calculate from the result of ash-analysis, the quantity of phosphoric acid required by a wheat crop, including grain and straw, we find the wheat demands more abundant supplies for phosphoric acid than any other plants. Wheat consumes phosphoric acid in greater quantities during the growth of the seed than at any other period ; and this is the time when practical men believe the soil to suffer the greatest exhaustion. Plants in general derive their carbon and nitrogen from the atmosphere ; carbon in the form of carbonic acid, nitrogen in the form of ammonia ; from water (and ammonia) they receive hydrogen ; and sulphur from sulphuric acid."

Boudrimont mentions the existence of interstitial currents in arable soils, and the influence they exert on agriculture. He states, "that there is a natural process at work by which liquid currents rise to the surface, and thus bring up materials that help either to maintain its fertility or modify its character." Many phenomena of agriculture and vegetation have at different times been observed, which, hitherto inexplicable, are readily explained on this theory ; such, for example, as the improvement that takes place in fallows ; and there is reason to believe that these currents materially influence the rotation of crops.

Take the masterly views of Schlieden, in Germany. He asserts that "the goodness of the soil depends on its inorganic constituents ; so far, at least, as they are soluble in water, or through continued action of carbonic acid, and the more abundant and various these solutions, the more fertile is the ground."

The amazing yield of Indian corn in Mexico, from two to six hundred fold, is something which, with all our skill, we cannot accomplish, and is a fact in favor of the argument, "that in no case do the organic substances contained in the soil perform any direct parts of the nutrition of plants."

All chemists are agreed as to the source from which the oxygen and hydrogen of plants are derived, the principal of which is water. All of them agree that the carbon of vegetables is derived principally from the air, partially from the soil. It becomes evident, then, from the most conclusive proofs, that *humus*, in the form in which it exists in soils, does not yield the smallest nourishment to plants. The excellent advantages derived from the experiments of talented and industrious men, who have directed every effort to aid practical agriculture, justly entitle them to golden praise from mankind. Liebig has the merit of having been the first who laid before the public some views as to the source of the constituents of plants. He remarks, "How does it happen that wheat does not flourish on sandy soil, and that a (calx or) calcareous soil is unsustainable for its growth, unless it is mixed with a large quantity of clay ? It is because these soils do not contain alkalies, and certain other ingredients, in sufficient quantity ; and, therefore, the growth of the wheat is arrested, even though all other substances should be present in abundance."

In some soils there may be too much straw-making food, but not enough for the maturing of the grain. When this is the case, even the most favorable seasons cannot give the best results. Again, the absence of the necessary moisture in the soil will cut off the supplies of food to plants. But an excess of it may cause available food wanting for the development of the grains to be appropriated to the straw. In very wet seasons, especially in the absence of under-drains, where there is much straw-making food and a deficiency of phosphates, the latter are taken up by the stalks and leaves, to the loss of the grain ; hence, some soils may yield less grain in a wet season, but more straw than they would do in a dryer one, other things being equal.

"Grain is carried to the cities, and the substances in the soil that made it, are removed far away from the original source, and the soil is robbed of it, and but a small portion of their elements are sent to the soil whence they were taken." In nature's economy nothing is lost ; but when man displaces things, he should put them back again in their own places. The wheat-grower should return to his lands, in the shape of fertilizers, the same elements which he has taken, or he will soon find the soil exhausted, so that he cannot produce the same grain. In many of our best wheat-growing places in the West, the lands are so much exhausted that wheat crops do not pay for their labor and expense of growing. The common opinion hitherto prevalent and still held by some, that the soil of the West cannot be exhausted, is, therefore, a great mistake.

In our cultivation of wheat we have exhausted the soil of so much of the elements that produce it, that maize is fast taking the place of wheat, especially in the prairie districts, where the ground is less protected by the snow in Winter than in others. In Canada, where the Winter is severe, the ground being covered by snow, the wheat does not suffer as that sown in more changeable climates. It is found by experience, that, in a climate where there is little snow, the land needs to be fertilized and plowed deep, in order to give the roots a strong hold in the soil. Fertilization will cause a vigorous growth, and the roots of plants, in well prepared soils, strike deep, and hold fast. This increases the growth of the plant, and augments the quantity and quality of the crops.

From the American Agriculturist.

BALKY HORSES.

The prime requisite for the successful management of a balky horse, is perfect *self possession* and patience, on the part of the driver. It is quite common to see men fly into a passion upon the first restive symptoms of the horse, and to deal out fierce punishment until compelled to desist, from sheer exhaustion, after which, when the driver has become calm, and the horse recovered from his fright, a start is effected and the trouble is over. Young horses, before they are completely broken, may stop when in the harness, from a feeling of inability to draw their load, from fatigue, from misunderstanding the will of the driver, or from an excitable disposition, leading them to act upon the impulse or the moment. In all these cases there is necessity for care and coolness in the driver. From the first, and for a long time, the load of a young horse should be such as he can draw with the greatest ease, thus giving him confidence in his own powers. A young horse once "set" will thereafter pull with uncertainty—hence with only half a will; he is then discouraged easily, and balks at trifling obstacles, or if he be of spirited disposition, he will spring to it with might and main, whenever he feels extra weight behind him, and if not allowed to work in this way will stop at once. It has been noticed that the worst balks usually occur at or near the foot of hills, and this may explain how the horse learns the habit. The driver should anticipate the wish of the horse to rest, by allowing even more frequent intervals than are required. This practice induces the habit of obedience, the horse willingly stops when the word is given, and thus is accustomed to heed the driver's command, which is the first and great requisite in his education. These commands should be given in a way that can readily be understood. A well trained animal shows remarkable intelligence in perceiving his master's wishes, but it is by long familiarity with his ways that this ability is acquired.

Balky horses are usually "high strung," possessing the very disposition, which, if properly treated, will give the best style and action. It is stated on good authority, that such horses may be so wrought upon by a single harsh exclamation, as to raise the pulse ten beats a minute. What wonder if such an animal should prove refractory upon suddenly feeling the lash of an infuriated driver. For this class of horses a whip need seldom if ever be used, when breaking them. They yield readily to kindness, and are as quick to obey when properly treated, as they are troublesome when "fooled" with—we use this term for want of a more expressive one. These remarks

apply more particularly to the prevention of balking, by proper management, of colts. When the habit of balking is fixed, impatience of the driver only increases the difficulty. The treatment then requires the highest common sense—the first thing men lose when they fly into a passion. The following directions, given by Mr. Rarey, are probably as sound and complete on this subject as anything ever published:

"Almost any team when first baulked, will start kindly, if you let them stand five or ten minutes, as though there was nothing wrong, and then speak to them with a steady voice, and turn them a little to the right or left, so as to get them both in motion before they feel the pinch of the load. But if you want to start a team that you are not driving yourself, that has been baulked, fooled, and whipped for some time, go to them and hang the lines on their hames, or fasten them to the wagon, so that they will be perfectly loose; make the driver and spectators (if there are any) stand off some distance to one side, so as not to attract the attention of the horses; unloose their check-reins, so that they can get their heads down if they choose; let them stand a few minutes in this condition until you can see that they are a little composed. While they are standing, you should be about their heads, gentling them; it will make them a little more kind, and the spectators will think that you are doing something that they do not understand, and will not learn the secret. When you have them ready to start, stand before them, and, as you seldom have but one baulky horse in a team, get as near in front of him as you can, and, if he is too fast for the other horse, let his nose come against your breast; this will keep him steady, for he will go slow rather than run on you. Turn them gently to the right, without letting them pull on the traces, as far as the tongue will let them go; stop them with a kind word, gentle them a little, and then turn them back to the left, by the same process. You will then have them under your control by this time: and as you turn them again to the right, steady them in the collar, and you can take them where you please."

From the Ohio Cultivator.

SELECTION AND BREEDING OF SHEEP.

Having taken a deep interest in Sheep Husbandry from my childhood, I have thought that the conclusions I have arrived at, from 20 years close observation, might be interesting to some, and I have concluded to write a few lines on that subject, for publication. There is no business that the farmers of this part of Ohio can pursue, which yields such an adequate return for the labor employed and capital invested, as wool-growing does. To make it profitable, the person engaged therein should know how to manage sheep, Winter and Summer, also something of their diseases and cures.

In starting a flock, if wool is the object, purchase of the most valuable sheep for that purpose, if they can be obtained at reasonable prices. It is better to pay $50 or $100 for a first-rate stock buck, than to use an inferior one at a much less price. This doctrine I am aware is contrary to the views of many of our farmers, nevertheless it is true. It is not within the means of every person wishing to get up a valuable flock of sheep, to purchase full bloods; to such I would recommend to purchase the best common ewes of the country, and grade them up with superior Spanish or Silesian rams.

In selecting ewes, shape, size and constitution are the main points that should govern the purchaser. For the improvement in quality and quantity of wool, they must look to the buck. I have spent hundreds of dollars in trying to get up a valuable flock of sheep, that I might have saved if I had known what experience has since taught me.— Thousands of highly fed grade sheep, with an artificial finish, have been shipped into our State, and sold as full bloods at enormous prices, by men possessing too good countenances to practice such rascality.

As soon as a mongrel reaches the point where he stamps his own likeness on his offspring, he is equally valuable, provided he is equal in other respects. The number of crosses that is necessary before it is fit to breed from a mongrel, is a disputed point amongst sheep-men. Some say four or five, others eight or ten. For my own breeding, the latter would be preferred. It sometimes happens that grade sheep produce wool equal to full breeds, but seldom produce stock of like quality. Persons who are not competent judges of a pure breed, are frequently much disappointed in purchasing such sheep for wool-growing purposes. Rams of high blood, possessing strong constitutions, are the most likely to stamp their own characteristics on their offspring. Hence the necessity of obtaining superior rams of this description to breed from.

The wool should be of even length and thickness all over the body—shortness and thinness on the sides and belly, are defects that should not be tolerated in a flock of sheep. It should densely cover the body all over, open in connected masses, presenting a glittering, white appearance, neatly crimped, possessing at the same time a plentiful supply of oil, to give the surface a dark appearance. Rams of this description, of superior form, are equal in value to a good farm stallion.

Persons who understand the true theory of breeding, are careful that ewes possessing defects are not bred to rams of like faults. If the ewe is a little too long legged, she should be bred to a shortish legged ram; if too thin fleeced, the ram should possess a thick, dense fleece; if the wool is too coarse and dry, the ram should be fine and oily. The defects of either buck or ewe should be met or counterbalanced by the decided excellence of the opposite sex. The farmers of Ohio might increase their wool in quality, and at least one-third in quantity, if they were careful to breed from none but the best of ewes. They would realize double the amount from their sale sheep that they do at present. Every farmer who owns 130 acres of cleared land, ought to realize an income of eight or ten hundred dollars annually, provided he has his farm stocked with a profitable kind of sheep, which can easily be accomplished by a judicious selection of rams to breed from.   NATHAN COPE.

Columbiana Co., Sept., 1859.

When you speak to a person, look in his face.

MIDGE, OR WEEVIL.

The following is an extract from a letter of John Johnson, of Geneva, N. Y.

All we want is a wheat that will be in full head about the 5th of June. Then the chaff gets too hard by the time the midge is ready, so that they cannot sting through the chaff. I see some writers, who think their brains *crammed* with science, say that they deposit the larvæ on the outside of the chaff, and that in four days it is alive, and creeps over the top of the chaff, and down to the young kernel of wheat; but I know better than that. I have watched them too often to believe any such nonsense. When the female gets full of the larvæ, or maggots, she is quite red in the body. She then sticks to the chaff, puts out her sting, and penetrates through the outer and *inner* chaff, and instinct teaches her to apply her sting right opposite the young wheat. If she happens to be above it, she pulls out her sting and tries lower. When she gets the place that answers her purpose, she sticks there for some time, and you can take hold of her with your finger and thumb, and pull out her stinger.— When she gets on a head that the chaff is too hard, she will move up and down the ear, trying every one; sometimes she will succeed on the very lowest kernels, and sometimes on the highest. If she don't succeed on any of them, she tries another ear.— They cannot stand a hot sun, and they seldom commence to sting the wheat until about two hours before sunset, and then they keep at their work of destruction until the dew falls. I have sat, with glasses on, amongst the wheat, for hours, watching them. I have never seen the midge, or fly, more numerous than this season, but the chaff of my red wheat, and the Missouri wheat, was altogether too hard for them, and it is only the very latest heads of the white wheat they could sting, and the loss from them is only trifling. I hope the Missouri wheat may yield as well or better than the Mediterranean, as the latter is only fit for poor, *worn* land. If the land is in good condition, it gets all down: hence a great loss and expense in harvesting. The Missouri wheat has a stiff straw, as stiff as the Soule's, and will stand up even, with extra manuring. There is very little wheat sown in this county. The Mediterranean was very good last year, and better this, and I think more will be sown this year, take the whole country.—*Ohio Farmer.*

STOCK-GROWING AT THE SOUTH.

The importance of devoting more attention than has hitherto been given to this branch of husbandry in all the cotton-growing region, is daily becoming more and more apparent. Intelligent agriculturists at the South are fully alive to the imperative necessity of providing, in some way, for the renovation of soils, naturally fertile, but exhausted by long continued cropping with cotton. The culture of grasses and the raising of stock, is nature's method of renovating the fields impoverished by long tillage, and this mode of treatment will be found, for the most part, efficient and economical. True, guano and artificial fertilizers may be resorted to, but will they thoroughly renovate the soil? We think it will hardly be claimed that more can be done with the aid of these fertilizers than to maintain a fruitful soil in its present condition. Other means must be resorted to, in order to restore to worn out lands their lost fertility.

The improvement of these by growing stock upon them, instead of being an item of expense, might, in most cases, with proper management, be made a source of profit. It is quite a common mistake to suppose that grasses will not flourish upon good cotton land. True, the clover and herds-grass of the Northern and Middle States will not flourish in a climate suited to the growth of cotton; but there are other grasses, such as the Kentucky Blue-grass, which would grow on any good soil, and will flourish on such as are rich in lime; the orchard-grass, &c., which will furnish excellent and abundant pasturage upon a great proportion of the exhausted cotton lands. That sheep, cattle, horses, and mules, can be profitably raised at the South has been abundantly shown by a vast number of successful experiments, and it is by many claimed that wool can be grown more profitably here than in any other section of the country. But we hear it said, "The cotton planter's business is to kill grass, instead of raising it—that cotton and stock cannot be profitably produced upon the same plantation, at the same time, that it is more profitable to wear out the land and go in search of virgin soil." May not the correctness of these sayings well be questioned? The growers of tobacco and hemp have found it profitable to connect stock-raising with the production of these staples; and we are confident the opinion is gaining ground among intelligent cotton planters, that it would be to their advantage to pay more attention to the improvement of the soil by stock-growing, thus increasing the amount of cotton grown per acre, and lessening the cost per pound of producing it.

Most kinds of stock could be grown at a very cheap rate upon a great proportion of the rolling cotton lands, which have become exhausted and are now of little value. The large sums now paid by the planter to other States for mules to work his crop, and bacon to feed his hands, would be saved; and while getting these at a cheaper rate he will be reaping from such a source a still greater advantage, in the greatly increased value of his lands.— We do not, for a moment suppose that a single acre of rich cotton fields, such as lie along the valley of the Alabama river, are to be devoted to stock-growing, so long as their fertility remains; nor do we wish to see the aggregate amount of the cotton crop diminish. On the contrary, we should prefer to see it increase, and this, we believe would be the sure result of judicious stock-growing upon the worn out soils.

Is not this a subject of grave importance, and worthy the careful consideration of every agriculturist at the South?—*American Stock Journal.*

From the Cotton Planter and Soil.

COTTON PACKING AND FALSE CONJECTURES OF THE CROP.

Dr. Cloud—*Dear Sir:*—I have two things to complain of, and they are against editors:

The first I will mention is, giving currency to the charges made against cotton planters for false packing cotton. Editors ought to know these charges are as groundless as Munchausen tales.— That there may be, out of the three-and-a-half millions of bales, some that are disgraceful to the packers, put up, we need not be surprised; but take half a million of people from any calling, let it be from the ministry even, or doctors, lawyers, I care not which, and you will find just as much rascality. You know the masses do not see their bales pressed, and even did they, it comes with a bad grace from certain quarters, when we take into count weights and measure returns—but I will not return slander for slander. Had I charge of a paper, the agriculturists of America would be the last men who should be charged with swindling in my paper, and of them all, I should stand up to cotton planters.

The other cause of complaint is, publishing the great prospects, "especially of the cotton crop," tickling every soft by heralding first bloom, first boll, and such like.

I ask planters, editors, all, who can tell what a crop will be in June, July, August, or even September? And look to the evil. The impression has already gone out that large crops of cotton are expected everywhere, and not the first are, that some planters on the Mississippi river were planting cotton in June! I have no objection to give to merchants and manufacturers the exact quantity made, but I do object to giving out so favorable reports, when the man lives not, who can, on the 1st day of August, make any certain estimate.

In 1844, I had a very excellent judge of the cotton crop to visit my little field, and we walked all about through it; he said it was "splendid;" "good for a bale per acre." This was in August, about the 25th, and to all appearances he was correct; yet, before the 10th day of September, my crop was not worth one-half bale per acre—I only made that much. Many of my neighbors do not make three hundred pounds of seed cotton per acre. All this is wrong; the cotton planters have enough to contend against without having their friends to work against them.

Yours with respect, S. T. N.
Jackson, Miss., 1859.

How to use Lime—Lime as a food for plants, is required in very small quantities, and for this purpose should be applied in very minute doses, and frequently. Shell lime is better than stone lime, *when wanted for manure.* When required not to feed plants, but to decompose other materials in the soil, such as inert organic matter, then larger doses may be given, and this should never be mixed with any manure of a nitrogenous kind—such as night-soil, phosphates, guano, or barn-yard manure.— Lime may be mixed with salt in the manner we have so often recommended, or with sour muck, or any other organic matter not readily decomposable. Never apply lime to the soil, within a day or two of the time when manure has been applied. When barn-yard manures have been deeply buried in the soil, a light top-dressing of lime may be used after the plowing. This will gradually sink, and when it meets with, and assists in decomposing the manure, the gases in rising, will be absorbed by the incumbent soil.—*The Working Farmer.*

THE WHEAT MIDGE.

A Mr. Dawson, of New York, thus relates his experience with the wheat fly:

"I procured a quantity of the larvæ, full-grown, in that motionless and torpid state in which they appear when the wheat is ripe. A portion of the larvæ were placed on the surface of wet soil in a flower-pot. In the course of two days the greater number of them had descended into the ground, previously casting their skins, which remained at the surface.

"I afterwards ascertained that they had penetrated to the depth of more than an inch, and were of a whitish color, softer and more active than they had previously been. The fact is thus established, that these apparently torpid larvæ, when they fall from the ripe wheat in fall, or are carelessly swept from the threshing-floor into the barn-yard, at once resume their activity and bury themselves in the ground.

"The larvæ, thus buried in the ground, were allowed to remain, undisturbed, through the winter and spring, the flower-pot being occasionally watered. About the end of June they began to re-appear above ground, in their winged form; the little grubs creeping to the surface, and projecting about half of their bodies above it, when the skin of the upper half burst, and the full-grown, winged midge came forth, and flew away. This completes the round of changes which this little creature undergoes, and we have thus actual evidence of each stage of its progress, from the egg to the perfect insect."

Mr. Dawson has recorded, also, that a friend of his informed him that not less than *four bushels of these insects had been obtained from the wheat of eight acres.*

Dr. W. J. Anderson, of Canada, reports as follows:

"When the maggot has been hatched early in the season, and finds the wheat in a favorable condition for its reception, it arrives at maturity before the harvesting, and, according to Professor Aind, 'leaves the grain at the close of a shower or heavy dew, and wriggles down the wet straw to the earth.'"

So far as our own observation has gone, it has satisfied us that as soon as the maggot has arrived at maturity, it does not attempt to leave the ear, but becoming stiff and torpid, either is shaken out by the waving of the corn in the wind, or by the process of harvesting, and thus reaches the ground. On arriving at the ground it is enabled by wriggling, or some other process, to bury itself there; it penetrates to the depth of more than an inch.—There is considerable difference of opinion as to the circumstances under which this takes place.

BUT ONE WAY TO FARM.

Hon. J. R. Williams, of Michigan, in his agricultural address, at the New York State Fair, at Syracuse, related the following anecdote:

"I met a man last year who, exultingly, declared that there was but one way to hoe—but one way to plow—but one way to harvest, and books and schools were, therefore, futile. If there is but one way to farm it, that is a very poor way, which affords an average crop of less than eleven bushels of wheat per acre, over such a country as we possess. This same friend called my attention to a Pennsylvania German, who could hardly read and write, and had a great contempt for papers and books on farming, but was the best farmer in his neighborhood. I told him that I thought the basket would not hold water, and that this model farmer owed everything to the spirit of improvement abroad. His plow was a Troy plow, instead of the old shaky implement, with a wooden mould-board sheathed with iron, with straight handles tipped with cow-horn, which he used when a boy. His implements were mostly light, graceful, elastic ones, of recent patterns. His fruit was budded and grafted from such as his neighbors had imported from the best nurseries. Whatever superior cattle, or sheep, or swine he had, were obtained from neighbors at no extra cost. The nails he shingled his house with cost but one-third as much as those which his father used. When he got up in the morning, he lighted his fire in a second with a friction match, instead of tugging ten minutes with flint and steel and tinder-box, and he complacently composed himself to sleep at night under sheeting that cost eight cents per yard, as good as that which cost fifty cents when he was a child. The story is told of Plato, that having described man to be a biped without feathers, Diogones, the cynic, laid a plucked rooster before him, and exclaimed, 'Behold Plato's man!' If our model farmer was deprived of all the benefits he had derived from that progress which he despised, if he was stripped of all borrowed plumes, he would be as innocent of feathers as Plato's man."

SHEEP HUSBANDRY IN THE WEST.

The following able and interesting article, written for the *Kentucky Farmer*, by R. W. Scott, late Secretary Kentucky Board of Agriculture, and one of the most successful sheep-growers in the country, is so worthy of consideration that we have been induced to publish it entire. It covers the whole ground and cannot be read without profit:

Sheep are among the most valuable domestic animals subjected to the use of man, feeding him with their flesh, clothing him with their wool, and enriching him by their rapid increase; and, although they do not either plow or draw for him, yet, by proper management, they will greatly assist him to clean the weeds, and briars, and bushes from his farm, as they will devour almost every green weed but the mullen and poke.

Though they do not appear to be of equal value in the West to the horse, or the cow, or the hog, yet it may be confidently asserted that in no other mode could our agricultural wealth be so suddenly and so greatly increased as by the general slaughter of dogs, which would certainly be followed by the universal introduction of sheep on the farms of our cultivated districts, and, also, by the dissemination of millions of them over the hilly and mountainous regions, and quickly wool would become one of our largest exports, and millions of acres of waste lands would be quadrupled in value, and would become a great source of revenue to the commonwealth.

But, notwithstanding the loss, vexation and insecurity occasioned by dogs, (which are the only obstacle to this unbounded success,) still, almost every farmer will find it advantageous to keep at least a few sheep; and the period of shearing is a good time to take a new, or an improved position on the subject. He who has no sheep should buy some now, and he who has some will find this the best time to improve them by selection, for now bad ones appear in all their "naked deformity," and the good ones are seen in unexaggerated excellence.

Every sheep which is in declining years, or is defective in size, form, thrift, or fleece, should now have a mark put upon it, and be put in process of preparation for being converted into mutton before the next winter.

An animal which will thrive in the open air, without shelter, with a constitution able to resist disease, and with power to cope with murderous dogs, with a large carcass of good mutton, clothed with a close and heavy fleece of wool of medium fineness—this is the animal which we want in sheep, and nothing short of this will meet the public taste. This we have already got; or, if we have not, we may certainly obtain it, for a skilful, careful and persevering breeder will find the animal almost as plastic in his hands, from generation to generation, as the potter does his clay.

In the selection of a breeding flock, the maxim that "like will produce its like," should be ever held in bright remembrance, and especially no male or female should be accepted which has the taint of hereditary disease upon it, for it will be, probably, transmitted to the offspring. Let the ewes be from one to five years old, with small heads, without horns, and with rather long and smooth faces, straight, broad backs, and full round bodies. The fleece should cover the whole body up to the face and forehead, under the belly, and down to the knees; and it should be as uniform, in length and fibre, over the whole body, as possible, and as free as possible from coarse and hairy locks on any part. A wavy appearance is not objectionable, but it should not amount to kinking and curling. A moderate degree of yolk is evidence of health, and is conducive to health by rendering the fleece impervious to rain, and it preserves the texture of the fibre; but an excess of it is exhausting to the animal, and promotive of foulness in the fleece, and should, therefore, be avoided.

During the summer the ewes should run apart from the bucks, and they should be frequently changed from one pasture to another, by which their fondness for roaming will meet with innocent indulgence; they will subsist almost entirely on weeds of different sorts, and on briars and bushes; and the health of the flock will be greatly promoted. When they begin to huddle together in the shade, and to hang their heads and stamp their feet for protection against the *sheep-fly*, additional exemption will be secured by smearing some tar on the forehead, and, also, on the nose, in the mucus of which the fly seeks to deposit her eggs.

They should at all times have access to salt, and the best plan is, to place it around the roots of some tree which you wish to kill, or some stump which you wish to extract. The salt is made more conducive to health by the occasional addition of sulphur, and also of wood ashes.

A tablespoonful of flour of sulphur and a pint of hog's lard mixed together, and a little of it smeared on the backs of each sheep, when the fleece is short, will be the best protection against ticks.

The ram should, if possible, be a paragon of excellence in every respect; for every quality which he has, good or bad, will be impressed, with almost unfailing certainty, upon his progeny. Those qualities of fleece or carcass which are the chief objects of the breeder, should, by all means, be developed in the ram in the highest degree, and they should be deeply implanted in his character. He should be not less than one year old, and should by no means be in declining life or health.

He should especially excel in the peculiar qualities of his breed, whatever they may be. He should have commanding size on masculine appearance, broad shoulders and rump, wide back, full, round body, deep brisket, and he should be covered all over with a full, close, uniform, soft and golden fleece; and be in all respects the best of his breed; and it should be remembered that breed or blood is of no value, except so far as it possesses and insures the qualities which are desired. When more than one ram is used in the same season, the ewes should be carefully selected, and be so bred that the superior excellence of each ram shall compensate, in the progeny, some fault or defect in the ewes; for example, the smallest ewes (other things being equal) should be bred to the largest ram, &c.

When two or more bucks are used in the same season, this precaution will be necessary to prevent a ram from being bred to his own progeny in future, which should never be done, if it is possible to avoid it, no matter how great is the excellence of the ram in question. Even after the ewes have all been bred and put together, it will be well to allow the best ram to continue for a while with the flock, for some ewe may have missed conception.

During gestation the ewes want no better keeping than the range of a woodland pasture, well set with blue-grass, with a fresh and plentiful allowance of stock fodder scattered on the ground to them every other day during the snows and cold of Winter; and during the severest weather they will need no other protection than their own fleeces, if they have been bred with systems and constitutions properly adapted to such treatment in this climate.

MANNER OF MILKING.

The manner of milking is a more powerful and lasting influence on the productiveness of the cow than most farmers are aware of. That a slow and careless milker soon dries up the best cows every practical farmer and dairyman knows. The first requisite of a good milker is, of course, the *utter cleanliness*. Without this the milk is unendurable. The udder should, therefore, be carefully cleaned before the milking commences. The milker may begin gradually and gently, but should steadily increase the rapidity of the operation till the udder is emptied, using a pail sufficiently large to hold all, without the necessity of changing. Cows are very sensitive, and the pail cannot be changed, nor can the milker stop or rise during the process of milking, without leading the cow, more or less, to withhold her milk. The utmost care should be taken to strip the last drop, and do it rapidly, and not in a slow and neglected manner, which is sure to have its effect on the yield of the cow. If any milk is left, it is re-absorbed into the system, or else becomes caked, and diminishes the tendency to secrete a full quantity afterwards. If gentle and mild treatment is observed and persevered in, the operation of milking appears to be one of pleasure to the animal, as it undoubtedly is; but if an opposite course is pursued—if, at every restless movement, caused, perhaps, by pressing a sore teat, the animal is harshly spoken to—she will be likely to learn to kick as a habit, and it will be difficult to overcome it afterwards. To induce quiet and readiness to give down the milk freely, it is better that the cow should be fed at milking time with cut food, or roots, placed within her easy reach. The same person should milk the same cow regularly, and not change from one to another, unless there are special reasons for it.—*Foreign Exchange.*

PUTTING IN FALL WHEAT.

There are various ways of plowing and seeding wheat, but there is to my notion but one right way. In traveling along you will see some setting ridges, some twelve, sixteen and twenty feet apart, upon which they haul their manure, and then go to work and plow out the remainder, leaving a very large dead furrow; then they spread the manure, leaving it all on the best ground, sow the wheat, and harrow it in.

Now, my way would be different: In the first place, I would haul the manure and plow it in as fast as I could conveniently, and, if the ground should be too hard for my team, I would put on more and then plow about ten inches deep, and in as wide lands as I could conveniently, and then harrow well, and, if the ground would do, roll it with a heavy roller, and then drill in about one-and-a-half bushels per acre.

This will not suit all farmers; they will say, if we do not plow in narrow lands, our wheat will all freeze out. But, if they would only take pains to plow deep, so as there is some hold for the roots, this need not be, if they only run water-furrows in places that need, which will drain their land much better than all their dead furrows, which only serve as reservoirs to hold water. But look at the wheat at harvest upon the two fields, and see the difference. In the one of narrow lands you will see very large straw on the middle of the land and on both sides there will be scarce any; thus only about one-third of the land produces wheat. In the field of wide lands, you will see it all over alike, not so rank as on the middle of the narrow lands, but take the same ground and there is one-third more wheat upon it, and when you come to reap it, if you do it with a machine, you can do it with some pleasure, and then you have a nice bottom for mowing the next year.

WM. K. MEAD.

From the Genessee Farmer.

SOWING WHEAT.

There is no question, in my mind, that drilling in seed wheat is, on all soils, better than broadcast sowing. So much greater a proportion of the seed is likely to germinate, that a much less quantity of grain is required to sow an acre. The use of a drill also saves all the labor of harrowing, where the soil is well prepared before-hand. In fact, it is better not to harrow the land after drilling in the wheat, as the slight ridges left by the drill are gradually crumbled down by the rain and frost, and form a protective covering to the young and tender plants in Autumn and Winter.

But every farmer cannot afford to buy so expensive an article as a drill machine, and some soils are too stony and cloddy to allow of its use. Others again are of a light sandy description. On such soils, broadcast sowing answers very well, if followed by the roller to crush the clods or render a light soil more compact, and prevent its washing by heavy rains. But on all well prepared loams, it is of no advantage to use the roller, the frosts of Winter performing the operation more gradually and beneficially; and on such soils the roller is of most benefit when used in the Spring; it then compresses the roots of the plants into the soil, after the disintegrating effects of the frosts are over. Wheat grown on a loamy soil, the surface of which is left very smooth and compact in the Fall, is liable to be Winter-killed by being heaved out in the Winter and early Spring by the frost, which, on a more ridgy and uneven surface, breaks down and crumbles the projecting soil. But on sandy soils, however compact they may be, who ever heard of wheat being Winter killed? The surface moisture that falls on such soils is too quickly absorbed for the frost to have time to produce any evil effect. A. B.

Charlotteville, C. W.

NIGHT SOIL—ITS VALUE.—The best of all manures is the one which, in our country, is the most universally wasted. In Belgium, where agriculture is carried to great productiveness, they "order things differently." There, the estimate is, by nice calculation, that it is worth $10 for every individual man, woman, and child. We traverse sea and land, send to Africa and South America to bring elements of fertility, which, at home, we throw away on every farm in the country. What an immense amount is wasted in our cities. It must be the most valuable, containing the elements of all kinds of food consumed by man, and, in returning these to the soil, we return the identical constituents which former crops and animals had taken from the land. Night soil contains the phosphate of lime, which is indispensable to the growth of animals, bones, and to the nutriment of all plants, and which is not supplied from the atmosphere like carbonic acid and ammonia. All fluid and solid excretions should be preserved by mixing with burnt clay, sawdust, ashes, peat, or wood charcoal, etc.

We have a great deal to learn, and, alas, much more to practice, that we have learned.—*Planters' Banner.*

The Farmer and Planter.

COLUMBIA, S. C., DECEMBER, 1859.

THE END OF VOLUME TEN---OUR FUTURE.

This number completes the first volume of the new series of the *Farmer and Planter.* How far we have succeeded in meeting the expectations of our citizens, we must leave to the judgment of those who have followed us monthly through the year. It is true, we have not pleased every one, but we did not expect to accomplish such an unheard-of feat, for, we think it would be reason for doubting the honesty and ability of those excellent gentlemen who have voluntarily and *gratuitously* devoted their time and talents to conduct a journal worthy, in every respect, the united support of this and the other Southern States. Our pages have not been polluted by fulsome and indiscreet puffs of untried plants, seeds, or other agricultural wonders, whereby so many of the planters and farmers have, of late years, been humbugged. Our object has been to instruct and elevate, not degrade, the agriculturists and their occupation. Had money, alone, been our polar star, the *Farmer and Planter* would have teemed with commendations of every nostrum that the most unscrupulous vendor ever invented, and the publisher's finances greatly improved. On the contrary, our aim has been, and ever will be, to warn the South against such impositions.

Our volume for 1860, will commence with a handsomely executed colored "Industrial Map of South Carolina," carefully prepared by OSCAR M. LIEBER, Esq., our very able State Geologist, whose writings have, during the past Summer, in the various District papers, given so much valuable information to our people, upon the capacities and resources of our State. This map will be found very valuable to every citizen of South Carolina, showing the boundaries of the Long and Short Staple Cotton, Indian corn, and small grains, and the mineral localities, as well as the forest growth of our State, &c., &c.

Other improvements to our journal will be made in accordance with the support it receives—a liberal support ensuring a liberal outlay. The present patronage is too meagre to allow of any outlay more than what is actually necessary for its punctual appearance.

Our arrangements are fully made for the issue of another volume ; but we candidly announce that, unless our subscription list *far exceeds* its present number, we shall discontinue it at the end of the *next year.* We give a year's notice of our intention, because we have determined not to refer to it again,

and with the hope that every friend of the journal will see the necessity of prompt action.

We would here state that the subscriptions of nearly all our subscribers expire with this number, and the journal will be discontinued to them, unless renewed. The cash system alone will be rigidly adhered to.—PUBLISHER.

THE FAIR.

The Fourth Annual Agricultural Festival of the good old Palmetto State has passed off with wonderful satisfaction. That ubiquitous individual, "everybody" did not take a premium—"everybody" did not have things go exactly as he wanted them, but he went home in a good humor, determined to do better, and come back next year a more earnest and formidable competitor. We had glorious weather.—How thankful should we feel for this fourth Providential smile upon our rural festival ! We had an immense concourse of people, we had good order, no accidents, no rows, quarrels, disorder or drunkenness—even the light-fingered gentry, who have picked everybody's pocket at all the Fairs in the country, did not dare to disturb the harmony of the Fair Grounds. We heard the remark made by a distinguished gentleman of another State, who had attended a great many Fairs during the year past, "that this was really the only rural festival he had ever been at—it bore everywhere upon its face, the unmistakeable impress of an agricultural people, bound together by common ties, and met together for common good." We put that down as the very highest compliment language is capable of expressing. And truly we have reason to be proud of a people who can meet together as competitors for prizes in the various departments of agriculture, without personal bickerings, envyings and suspicions—who can return to their homes gratified, and determined to meet again, better prepared to carry off the prize.

NOMENCLATURE.

"Let things be called by their right names."

Among the greatest faults of our Agricultural people, may be reckoned their carelessness about applying the proper names to seeds, plants and fruits.

A grape, apple, or peach, a variety of wheat, corn or cotton, takes the name of some individual who has cultivated it successfully, and has a run. The planter hears its virtues lauded—puts himself to much trouble to procure it, and, after making an especial pet of it, finds out he has only been nursing a favorite long since given up for a new candidate. Under how many different names do we find our favorite Carolina Grape, the Lenoir, Black July, Devereaux, Ohio, &c. So with our apples and peaches.

During the last five or six years, our farmers have been devoting a good deal more of their attention to wheat culture, and several new varieties have come into notice. We hear of the Gale, the Tubman, the King, the Mogul, the Walker, the Motte, the Blue-Stem, the Tuscan, the Tappehannock, the Orleans, the Reaphook, the Alabama, &c. How many of these may be the same wheat, is a matter well worth being settled. Will some of our wheat friends see to it?

HORSES.

"He smelleth the battle afar off, the thunder of the Captains and the shouting."

We cannot too earnestly direct the attention of our readers to the improvement of the breed of this invaluable animal. The high prices now demanded everywhere for fine animals afford abundant evidence of the importance of our devoting more time and *system* to their breeding.

We have the best blood to begin with. Let us take the right cross and use the right means, and we may soon be independent of the world.

BRAHMINS.

The popularity of this newly imported breed of cattle seems to be rapidly on the increase, notwithstanding the opinion of many of the Croaker family. The high price at which they have been generally held, has, doubtless, been in their favor, as it has kept them in the hands, mainly, of judicious breeders, who have crossed them upon good animals.

So far as our experience goes, nearly all *crosses* from a well-bred animal upon an inferior race, are an improvement. We have been particularly struck with one fact, that the Brahmin makes his mark more decidedly than any breed we know of. His crosses upon the Durham make very beautiful animals, and much more thrifty ones than the Durham proper. There can be no doubt about their hardiness, their thrift, their activity, and their bottom. They must make admirable oxen. Their docility has been questioned, but without cause, if any reliance can be placed in the very interesting statement published in our present issue, from the pen of a distinguished writer in the *American Stock Journal*. It will be seen by this account, that we have been fortunate in getting the purest blood to begin with.

STRAW---ITS VALUE AS FOOD.

At a recent meeting of the London Farmers' Club, the above topic was very fully discussed. Mr. Mechi stated that 100 lbs of straw contained the equivalent of 15 lbs of oil. From analysis by a distinguished professor in an English agricultural college, the estimate of Mr. Mechi is more than sustained.—

His estimates have been published in Morton's Cyclopedia of Agriculture, where it is stated that each 100 lbs of wheat straw, contains 72 per cent. of muscle, fat, and heat-producing substances; of which 27 per cent. are soluble in potash, and 35 per cent. insoluble. "The soluble fattening substances are equal to 13½ lbs of oil in each 100 lbs of straw."

Mr. Mechi has been one of the most successful farmers in Great Britain, and it is worth remarking, that he left the beaten track at the beginning, struck out a new course for himself, and allowed nothing to arrest his exertions until he achieved success. He is now admitted on all hands as good authority.

On how many farms in the country do we find the straw taken care of. Even sensible people will tell you that "there is no strength in it," it will make your cattle lousy, give them the hollow horn, and all such nonsense.

Take care of your straw—sprinkle a little salt amongst it, when you stack or house it, and it will pay better as food than mulch upon poverty knobs.

CONCENTRATED MANURES.

Everybody who has been in the habit of looking over the columns of the Agricultural press for a few years past, must have been struck by the wonderful increase in the manufacture of concentrated fertilizers. It is a question well worth solving, whether this increase is owing to the popularity or value of the manure, or to the *profits* which go into the pockets of the manufacturers? It is a question not easily answered, for one man will tell you that Mr. A's fertilizer is a humbug, and will not pay; while another will give the fertilizer a certificate of infallibility. We have not much faith in the idea that manufacturers of these manures are actuated, *solely*, by a devotion to the agricultural prosperity of the country. They promise too much for ordinary credulity, and they are altogether too anxious to sell for people who are doing a losing business. It is next to impossible that the results claimed by them, to follow the use of their manure, should be true. It is little short of nonsense to assert, that a soil, exhausted by years of reckless culture, could be restored, or made to yield remunerative crops, by the addition of a few spoonfuls of bone-dust, ammonia, or lime.

Dr. Emmons says, in a Report, that ordinary analysis exhibited but a trace of Phosphate of Lime in the soil of Wheatland, New York; and yet, it is known to be one of the best wheat soils in the country, which has produced fine crops for many years. The mania just now for Phosphatic manures seems to be very great; every paper is full of puffs and advertisements; agents are perambulating the country, and agencies established everywhere amongst us. It is well enough to look a little into the business. The sensible communication of "Hygeia," in our November No., is suggestive, and it may be not only well enough to ask the Phosphatic manufacturers, not only how they make their Sulphuric Acid, but where they get their bone-dust? Pure bone-dust, we have seen it stated in the papers, is an article not easily procured.

We have dabbled enough in Phosphatic manures to be convinced that there is uncertainty, adulteration, or *something* that interferes with their value as a fertilizer.

As it is our determination to protect, as far as we can, the agriculturist against all impositions, or humbugs, we have thought proper to throw out the above hints.

A SOUTH CAROLINA MOLE-TRACK NORTH OF MASON AND DIXON'S LINE.

Our readers will find in our present number a capital article, from the *Working Farmer* on the subject of plowing. There can be no doubt of the fact that the greatest difficulty in our path is our bad plowing.

We can never improve our soils permanently without we can go down into them and render available the salts which lie dormant in them.

We never will take the time to do it, and, in fact, we never could do it with the plows in common use upon our plantations. Whether Prof. Mapes' plows will do all he says for us, is a question well worth testing. His success in growing maximum crops upon the red kellis hard-pans of New Jersey speaks very loudly in his favor.

It is a little remarkable that all this wondrous improvement in the "Reversible Lifting Subsoil Plow" and Mole Plow, is nothing more nor less than the Subsoil Plow, exhibited at our Fair by our friend R. A. Springs—the idea of which our Yankee cousins got from a cut in the *Farmer and Planter* years ago.

Some people have not only a genius for invention, but for appropriation.

COUNTRY vs. CITY.

The want of laborers in the field of agriculture seems to be acknowledged from Maine to Texas.—Notwithstanding the immigration from abroad, and our natural increase at home, the rural population is constantly decreasing, and the supply of food, as a matter of course, does not keep pace with the demand. The people in the United States seem to have a proclivity to settle in the towns. Mr. GREELEY says, that more than half of the people of Illinois live in the cities and large towns. Illinois is looked upon as one of our purely agricultural States. It is as fertile as a garden, and a new country to boot.

A sensible writer in the *Country Gentleman*, of N. Y., says, that nine-tenths of the increase in the population of New York, for the last fifteen years, has been in the cities and large towns; that, while the whole State has increased in population more than 40 per cent., thirteen of the counties, almost entirely *agricultural*, have decreased. This is a remarkable state of things; but if we will carefully examine our own condition, in the old Southern States, the same work is going on, slowly but surely. Every day we are losing more and more of our rural population—the steady, working portion of it, and their farms are being absorbed by the cotton plantation. We are rapidly drifting to the condition, when the only poor folks we will have amongst us will be those we can't run off or buy out—who expect to live by traffic with our slaves.—This is the most dangerous element in our society, and the more carefully it is looked to, and the sooner and more rigidly the laws are enforced, the safer and the better.

It is the true policy of the South to bind together, as closely as possible, the interests and sympathies of the working classes and the slaveholder, and, above all, the working classes of our rural population. The late outbreak at Harper's Ferry, and efforts to bring about insurrection, points but too plainly to the classes in which such efforts will begin. We are an agricultural people; it is our duty to educate our children with a view to that; to infuse into them a belief that it is an honorable and fascinating occupation; to discourage them in that disposition to flock to cities and villages, and engage in professions already filled with drones; to point out to them the dangers that beset the path of youths in towns and cities, and show them the loafers, loungers, drunkards, and gamblers, about the streets, that have been manufactured out of sound, healthy, promising young men, who went to town to become gentlemen. There is a screw loose somewhere, and we are inclined to think it is about the *Hearthstone*.

THE GUANO CONTROVERSY.

A very interesting discussion has been going on for some time in one or two Agricultural journals of the country, upon the adulterations and monopoly of Guano. Some facts have leaked out that may be well enough for the planter to have an eye to in his purchases for the next year. We have it from good authority, that the adulteration of Guano has been reduced to a business; it is mixed to suit the seller's interest—not the purchaser's. If you want a low-priced article, you can get it; if you want a good article you must run the risks. The truth of the matter is, chemistry has made such wonderful advances, that there is hardly anything which can-no the imitated so well as to deceive the best judges. The liquors you drink, the wines you sip, the perfumes you inhale, your coffee, your tea, your flour, sugar, bread and butter, are all, more or less, adulterated ; and the shrewd chemist can make so good an imitation out of his chemicals, that it requires no ordinary skill to detect the imposition ; and this can be done so cheaply, that there is no wonder that a very brisk business is done in it.

You cannot be too cautious about laying out your money for Guano. There is no doubt of the fact, that nearly all the Guano now in the United States is owned by a company which has power to exact its own price while the demand continues so great; and as long as the price keeps up, the temptation to palm off new varieties of Guano, and adulterate the genuine Peruvian, will be too great to be resisted.

In our conversations with planters from various portions of the State, we have been puzzled to account for the different results of Guano application. Upon soils of exactly the same character, in the same neighborhood, and under the influence of the same seasons, the results have been very different. It cannot be accounted for upon any other principle than adulteration. Monoply is bad enough ; but one can refuse to buy, and, perhaps, bring the seller to terms; but when you never know what you are buying, or on whom you can rely, it is a matter of more serious difficulty. Keep your eyes open ; the increase in consumption of Guano during the past season, will introduce a great many *improved* varieties—fill the newspapers with chemical-analysis advertisements, and the country with fancy manure-drummers.

WASTE OF FERTILIZERS.

We are in the habit of talking a great deal about the want of fertilizers for our exhausted fields, while we take less pains than any people on the globe to save from waste, the heaps of fertilizing substances daily accumulating about our dwellings, only to putrify and generate disease.

One cannot take a step in any direction without the nose being offended by abominable odors, arising from various materials undergoing decomposition, which might, by a small outlay, be neutralized and converted into valuable fertilizers. Cities are the great wasters of fertility—the fruits of the earth are therein consumed in the greatest abundance, while nothing is saved to be returned to the soil from which the fruits were taken.

The slops of the kitchen, the sweepings of the yard, the night-soil, nearly everything of the kind, is carried off in the sewers, or transported to some out-of-the-way point to fill up gullies, and generate disease. This is miserable economy, and it is no wonder that our lands are daily growing poorer and poorer under such a system. Nothing should be lost which can be saved. Nothing should be wasted or misapplied, which can economically be converted into manure—and there are very few things which cannot. A small outlay for charcoal dust, plaster, a small supply of clay or muck, will enable one to convert an incredible amount of offensive matter into good manure.

It will be found not only good economy to do it, but it will be found conducive to our health and our comfort.

A little more attention to this subject, and we will not be so dependant for concentrated manures, upon our ingenious friends of the laboratory. Below may be found a recipe for making a very cheap guano, which will be found superior to many of those so highly puffed by the manufacturers :

ARTIFICIAL GUANO.—I enclose a recipe for a new fertilizer, which I intend preparing this week, by way of trial. The cost of the raw material is about $10.

VALENTINE'S RECIPE FOR ARTIFICIAL GUANO.

No. 1. Dry Peat,	20	bushels.
No. 2. Wood Ashes,	3	"
No. 3. Fine Bone Dust,	3	"
No. 4. Calcined Plaster,	3	"
No. 5. Nitrate Soda,	40	pounds.
No. 6. Sulphate Ammonia,	33	"
No. 7. " Soda,	40	"

If peat cannot be obtained, use garden mould or clean virgin soil.

MIXING.

Mix Nos. 1, 2 and 3 together ; then mix Nos. 5, 6 and 7 in four or five pails of water : when dissolved, add the liquid to the mixture of 1, 2 and 3, as in making mortar: when thoroughly mixed, add No. 4, the calcined plaster, which will absorb the liquid and bring the whole to a dry state.

Mix under cover, in a dry place. Pack so as to exclude air.

Product, one ton, which will manure 7½ acres of land.

I think the Artificial Guano would be improved by the addition of a bushel each of poudrette and dried blood, and shall try its effect.

IMPROVED FARMING.

We clip the following suggestive hints from the correspondence of the *American Farmer.*

The writer seems to know what are the deficiencies in the older Southern States, and to be confident that they can be supplied easily and economically, by pursuing the proper course. The man who can point out that course, and make the people believe in it, will be looked upon as a public benefactor. " *It can't be done with Peruvian guano ;* and the sooner the farmers find it out the better for them." Mark that, reader :

"I wish you could see this part of our country; there is no finer in the Union. It adjoins the lower part of Cecil. Twenty-five years ago nearly three-fourths of it was in commons—turned out—worn down—and sold at five and three dollars per acre.—There are thousands of acres in Delaware still much like it was, but there is a general waking up here *now*. There are very large quantities of such land in Maryland and Virginia. All, above water, in the old States South, can be brought up, like ours, from five to an hundred dollars per acre.

It can't be done with Peruvian guano; and the sooner the farmers find it out the better for them.—Clover, plaster, lime, *will do it*—has done it for us, and our soil and climate is much like that of the States named. It won't do to *burn* off the clover; nor to keep an over stock to eat it all off, no, no!—I've seen two tons per acre turned under—harrow and roll, time and again, if necessary—and I've seen thirty bushels of wheat cut from the acre, after such farming.

"SANDED COTTON."

We call attention to the communication of "A Planter," clipped from the *Mercury*, on the above subject.

A great deal of fuss is annually made about fraudulent packing of cotton—as usual, all the sins are pushed back upon the planter's shoulders. Cotton may lie on the platforms of railroads, be tumbled over the dust and dirt of wharves, be exposed to the rain for months, be tumbled into the hold of the vessel amidst all manner of trash, and no damage is done to it. Collect what it may, in the way of dust, dirt and water, on its travel, it is all to be charged to the design of the planter to defraud. It may be torn to pieces, ropes may be broken, bagging rent—it's all the planter's fault. The sin is at his door.—Sanded Cotton! What nonsense! The planter strains every nerve, drops all farm work, to pick his cotton out before a storm beats it out—it is his interest to do so, and if a storm comes and injures it, so as to make the buyer offer a low price, the planter is abused for sanding his cotton. We have heard factors say that very often the soiled cotton was really the best staple, and would command more in the English market than the whitest sample, picked before the rain, yet the planter had to sell it a cent less per pound. If anything is made by the operation, we are sure it is not by the planter—he accounts for the sand in the *weighing* and in the *price*.

From the Charleston Mercury.

"SANDED COTTONS."

I noticed in a telegraphic dispatch in your issue of Friday last, that the Manchester Chamber of Commerce had addressed the American Chamber, upon the subject of "Sanded Cotton;" and I have also observed several extracts published in your paper from Liverpool and New Orleans papers, denouncing the practice of "sanding" cotton by planters, as a huge fraud and disgraceful cheat. I would agree with these *well-informed* writers in their eloquent invectives, if there existed the least reason for their denunciations. But the truth is this, and it is patent to every planter, that no one in his senses, or who had any idea of his pecuniary interest, would resort to this imputed practice. If the planter had any earnest and determined desire to sink money, he might resort to this practice—not otherwise. When fine cotton commands 12½ cents in your market, "sanded" will not bring more than seven cents, a difference of more than twenty dollars on every bale. It is utterly impossible that a planter could put sand enough in his cotton to overbalance this difference in price, without certain detection. I have no doubt of the existence of "sanded cotton," and in great abundance, too, and I am not surprised to learn that three hundred thousand bags of the stock on hand in England is of this description, but it is easily accounted for, and without imputing fraud to the planter.—Throughout the pine woods region of our State, which are our best and most certain lands—and I believe the remark I am about to make is true of this character of soil throughout the cotton-growing States—the cotton opens early and rapidly during the months of August and September, and is subject to the beatings and peltings of the heavy rains and storms peculiar to that season. The soil being light and porous, and withal very black, the same spatters upon the cotton, beats it out, and sometimes even into the soil, and it never can be made to look decent again. It is astounding what amount of sand can be driven into the cotton by this cause, and it can only be gotten out by means of the "screen," a machine almost entirely abandoned, because the cotton buyers pronounced its use to be injurious and destructive to the staple.—Last winter I used the "screen" upon a lot of 12,000 lbs of seed cotton, (storm cotton) and I really believe that the amount of sand knocked out by this machine would have proved a good load for a four-horse team on a fair road. I did not realize for it, in your market more per pound than I did for other storm cotton, not "screened," sold at the same time, because, as the buyers say, the staple is injured by the screen; and, besides, the color of the cotton is against it. But we defraud no one in this matter. The cotton shows for itself as "storm cotton," and, of course, we have to take low prices. The season for gathering has been so good this fall that there will be very little sanded cotton; but there always has been some, and always will be some, sent to market, and the manufacturer will always be glad to buy it until that long-looked-for (by the manufacturer) "good time coming," but never reached, and never to be reached until the British government opens India to the African slave trade—when the supply of cotton will exceed the demand.

A PLANTER.

For the Farmer and Planter.

HORSES.

The value of horses in Ohio is estimated at about $40,000,000. Ten years ago it was $16,000,000.—We very well remember, when the railroad argument was in full vogue, one of the grand reasons given for encouraging the construction of railroads, was that it would do away with the use of horses, and thus cut down the expenses of the plantation. Has it had that effect? Has the increase in horses not kept pace with the increase in population? And what is the cause of it? Is it owing to injudicious breeding, to the want of food, to diseases, or is it because fast men must have fast horses, and fast horses, like fast men, as the jockey said, "soon run their capital out." Or is it owing to the mania for breeding mules? How many men reflect upon the fact that a mule's increase stops with the mules—that a mule's place can only be supplied by bringing another, and that the raising of mules has the effect of enhancing the price of both mules and horses?—Let every small farmer get a mare and try to raise a good horse colt as an experiment.

SNAFFLE.

For the Farmer and Planter.

HOG PENS.

Mr. EDITOR :—The season for penning hogs for fattening is drawing nigh. As soon as your hogs have picked the peas off your fields, put them in close pens, large enough for a sleeping and eating apartment. Fill up well, with leaves, weeds, or any kind of litter, the sleeping apartment, and protect the hogs from cold winds and rains—for this, you may use boards, pine tops, corn-stalks, &c.

Give your hogs salt, ashes, charcoal and, now and then, pine top tea. If they do not seem to be thriving, soak their corn in copperas-water occasionally.

Peas, pumpkins, soaked corn, slops—everything you can fix up, in the way of food, to save the corn-crib. When the litter in the pen is cut up, replenish. Ditch round the pen to keep water out.

It is incredible what a quantity of manure a hog will make, if kept at work properly. As soon as you get him fat, and the weather is cold enough, kill him and cure him. The only way to be sure of good bacon, is to cure it and store it, before the warm days in January or February come round.

HOG AND HOMINY.

For the Farmer and Planter.

THE FAIR.

Mr. EDITOR :—Every friend of Agricultural progress must have been gratified by the late Exhibition. There was not only a manifest improvement in many of the departments, but a decided improvement in the tone of the people. The competition was of the right spirit, and, with very few exceptions, the desire seemed to be more to demonstrate *what* is best than *mine* is best. That is the right spirit—in fact, the only spirit that can ever make a people great or a State prosperous.

If I have not the best breed of animals, the best variety of cotton, corn, wheat, the best cotton gin, plough or wagon, the sooner I know it the better; and there is no way by which we can sooner become aware of the fact than by fair competition before disinterested judges. No people ever attained greatness in any pursuit by pursuing the Chinese policy of thinking they had all that was best.

Our people are just beginning to comprehend the uses and the importance of these Fairs, and every new contributor, every new visitor, will find something to interest and improve him, while he will go home surprised at the resources, the ingenuity and the wonderful variety of tastes existing among a people peculiarly Agricultural in their tastes, and naturally averse to displays and exhibitions.

The Ladies' Department could not boast of as large a display and as great a variety; but we are told by many excellent judges, among the ladies, that the specimens of work were more beautiful and ingenious. We heard the remark made by gentlemen who had attended Fairs in many other States, that they had never seen as many beautiful specimens of original work—that everything bore the mark of being made at home, and designed to represent the idea of a rural or domestic population.

This was certainly a high compliment, and suggests to the Executive Committee the propriety of erasing from their Premium List "French and Spanish Needle Work, &c."

In the Fine Arts we had a goodly number of exhibitors. We would like to see more originality in this department. There can never be much improvement so long as one confines himself to be the mere copyist of some old master. We confess to belong to a school of Nature, and would take more pleasure in gazing upon a rude landscape, with strong points, sketched "to the life" with a bold pencil, or a mere outline of the face divine, speaking for itself, boldly and fearlessly, than in musing over the imaginings of a Ruben, Murillo, or Domenichian, for a week. In the department of Ivorytypes, Photography, &c., a great improvement was manifest in the beautiful productions of Messrs. Wearn & Hix.

In the department of Field Crops there was a great improvement. There were four competitors registered for the largest production of cotton per acre. There were several competitors for largest yield of corn per acre. This has been a bad corn year, and the yield of ears is not remarkably good. Five competitors for wheat, ranging from 56 bushels of wheat to 20 bushels per acre. There were five competitors on hay—Dr. Crook, of Greenville, one of our most zealous grass advocates, bore off the prize for the best clover hay, a most astonishing crop—6,940 lbs 1st mowing, 6,000 lbs, 2d mowing. Some beautiful specimens of native grass hay were on exhibition.—There were also some fine specimens of pea-vine hay. The premium for the largest yield of Pea-Vine Hay, was awarded to Maj. Theo. Starke, Columbia, yield being immense. The specimens of Field Peas were remarkably good; better than any previous exhibition. And so it may be said of everything but Oats, in that Department.

The Household Department was well filled by the ladies, and the specimens were remarkably good.—The butter show was admirable—very far above anything on exhibition heretofore. The show of bread was very good, and, we should take it, very much enjoyed—certainly a compliment to the exhibitors. The show of fruits, for the season, was very good; the specimens and varieties of native seedlings annually improve and increase.

The exhibition of Farming Implements was large and attractive. The common defect, so long apparent in all improved implements *for the South*, was still manifest—a mark of simplicity. The more simple the construction of an implement, the better its adaptation to the negro. Perfection will soon be knocked into fits by their hands, and the very moment a fellow proclaims that he has a perfect implement, you hear the practical planter say "humbug!" Improvements are being daily made in cotton gins, seed planters, sowers, cotton-presses and plows, and we may expect, from these exhibitions, the inventive genius of our own people will soon be turned in the right direction, and strike out something adapted to our own wants. The Peeler Plow, a Southern invention, from its simplicity and success, bids fair to be recognized as an improvement in the right direction. It received a premium at the late Fair. We understand that it is the intention of the Executive Committee to have the trial of plows, hereafter, conducted upon better principles. The great interest evinced in the matter, and the importance of knowing the truth, call for the greatest care and the best of judgment on the part of the Committee to which it is entrusted.

The Machine Department was very well filled, and many things exhibited in it deserving close examination.

The Horse show was admirable—about 170 animals were on exhibition, we are informed, and among them some of the very finest. We were pleased to see several fine Morgan stallions and mares on the list.

The exhibition of Sheep was superior to any former one. We had some fine Cotswold, Merinos, Southdowns, Leicesters, &c., some of them imported.

The show of Hogs was considerably better. Some very fine animals, from the large Litchfield and Lincoln, down to the thrifty Essex, as well as some new importations of English Grass Hog and Yorkshire.

The Cattle show was very fine. The Devons were as beautiful as ever. There were some superb Durhams—some new importation; a great increase and improvement in the Ayrshires, as well as in the grades and natives. The exhibition of Brahmins was remarkable. There is no cross which seems to tell so wonderfully. Be it made on whatsoever breed it may, it is sure to come out a Brahmin.

The Executive Committee have been enabled, by the liberality of the City Council, to make some very great improvements. The Saloons for the Ladies were very important additions, and the Amphitheatre, by its crowded condition, afforded the best evidence of its popularity. It was the admiration of everybody.

Nor can too many thanks be returned to the City authorities, and the citizens of Columbia, for their successful efforts to accommodate the visitors. They have retrieved their character.

A LOOKER ON.

FIRE PROOF COMPOSITION TO RESIST FIRE FOR FIVE HOURS.—Dissolve, in cold water, as much pearlash as it is capable of holding in solution, and wash or daub with it all the boards, wainscoting, timber, &c. Then diluting the same liquid with a little water, add to it such a portion of fine yellow clay as will make the mixture the same consistence as common paint; stir it in a small quantity of paperhanger's flour paste, to combine both the other substances. Give three coats of this mixture. When dry, apply the following mixture: Put into a pot equal quantities of finely pulverized iron filings, brick dust and ashes; pour over them size or glue water; set the whole near a fire, and when warm stir them together. With this liquid composition, or size, give one coat; and on its getting dry, give it a second coat. It resists fire for five hours, and prevents the wood from ever bursting into flames. It resists the ravages of fire so as only to be reduced to coals or embers, without spreading the conflagration by additional flames; by which five clear hours are gained in removing valuable effects to a place of safety, as well as rescuing the lives of all the family from danger! Furniture, chairs, tables, &c, particularly staircases, may be so protected. Twenty pounds of finely sifted yellow clay, a pound and a half of flour for making the paste, and one pound of pearlash, are sufficient to prepare a square rood of deal boards. When the Chinese were told the risk we ran of being roasted alive in our many storied mansions, they remarked: "What little land the English must possess, that compels them to build such high houses!"

POULTRY.

An idea prevails with many that any sort of grain, even if a little damaged, will do for poultry; but this is a great mistake. A friend of the writer once came very near losing his whole flock of valuable fowls, from feeding them with damaged corn, which had been heated. Those who feed largely know better, and invariably make it a rule to feed none but the best, and, if of corn, it is all the better for being broken.

There is just as much necessity of breeding from birds that are good layers, as in selecting milch cows those animals which are bred from good milkers, though, as in fowls, it does not necessarily always follow that their progeny are equally profitable.

The floor of the house should be of any material easily scraped clean; quick lime and coal ashes mixed and put on hot, bind well, and if coated with boiled tar when dry, will be found to stand well.—Bricks have been recommended by some, but they are objectionable on account of their absorbing moisture.

A barrel of fowl manure, mixed with muck or leaf mold, will manure half an acre of corn, and is as valuable as guano. The dung of poultry contains silica, and phosphate and carbonate of lime; and, along with pigeon dung, has been dried and broken down, pounded, and mixed with earthy substances, and applied in moist weather, and covered by harrowing of the seed, at the rate of forty or fifty bushels of the mixture to the acre. If used fresh, the quantity must be small; but, as a very small quantity of such excrements will come into possession of the farmer, the readiest and, probably, the most economical application will be to spread it evenly on the top of a dung heap, just before its being turned over, which will mix the substances, and extend the benefits equally.

Like human beings, fowls are susceptible of being influenced by change of climate, dirt, soil and water. They require a little care until they become acclimated, which they never fail to be after a time; but it is unfair to condemn them as tender, or unfitted for any particular locality, because a trial of a few months has not been satisfactory. The habits should also be studied. Some bear confinement without injury—others require a range. Their properties are so different, that every one may be suited if he will only take the necessary trouble and seek proper information.

TO KEEP BUTTER HARD AND COOL.

A writer in the *Scientific American* recommends to the ladies a very simple arrangement for keeping butter nice and cool in the hottest weather: Procure a large, new flower-pot, of sufficient size to cover the butter plate, and also a saucer large enough for the flower-pot to rest in upside down; place a trivet or meat stand (such as is sent to the oven when a joint is baked) in the saucer, and put on this trivet the plate of butter; now fill the saucer with water, and turn the flower-pot over the butter, so that the edge will be below the water.—The hole in the flower-pot must be fitted with a cork; the butter will then be in what we may call an air-tight chamber. Let the whole of the outside of the flower-pot be then thoroughly drenched with water, and place it in as cool a place as you can. If this be done over night, the butter will be as "firm as a rock" at breakfast time, or, if placed there in the morning, the butter will be quite hard for use at tea time. The reason of this is, that when water evaporates, it produces cold; the porous pot draws up the water, which, in warm weather, quickly evaporates from the sides, and thus cools it; and as no warm air can now get at the butter it becomes firm and cool in the hottest day.

Some Hints about Butter.—A good brine is made for butter, by dissolving a quart of fine salt, a pound of loaf sugar, and a teaspoonful of saltpetre in two quarts of water, and then strain it on the butter.—Packed butter is most perfectly preserved sweet by setting the firkin into a larger firkin, and filling in with good brine, and covering it. Butter will keep sweet a year thus.

Buttermilk kept in potter's ware, dissolves the glazing, and becomes poisonous.

Never scald strainers or milk vessels till thoroughly washed, as the milk or cream put in them will be injured by it. The best way to scald such vessels is to plunge them all over into scalding water, and then every spot is scalded.

Butter will sometimes not come because the air is too much excluded from the churn.

COMPARATIVE VALUES.—Experiments, and close and careful comparison of the results of many trials, have given the following as the comparative difference between the articles mentioned and hay;—

100 pounds of hay is equal to
275 pounds of green Indian corn,
442 pounds of rye straw,
164 pounds of oat straw,
153 pounds of pea straw,
201 pounds of raw potatoes,
339 pounds of mangel wurtzel,
504 pounds of turnips,
54 pounds of rye,
46 pounds of wheat,
59 pounds of oats,
45 pounds of peas or beans,
57 pounds of Indian corn,
68 pounds of acorns,
105 pounds of wheat bran,
109 pounds of rye bran,
167 pounds of wheat, pea, and oat chaff,
179 pounds of rye and barley.

RECEIPTS FOR TESTING EGGS.—There is no difficulty whatever in testing eggs; they are mostly examined by a candle. Another way to tell good eggs is to put them in a pail of water, and if they are good they will lay on their sides, always; if bad, they will stand on their small end, the large end always uppermost, unless they have been shaken considerably, when they will stand either end up.—Therefore, a bad egg can be told by the way it rests in water—always end up, never on its side. Any egg that lies flat is good to eat, and can be depended upon. An ordinary mode is to take them into a room moderately dark, and hold them between the eye and a candle or lamp. If the egg be good, that is, if the albumen is still unaffected, a light will shine through a reddish glow; while, if affected, it will be opaque or dark.—*Springfield Republican.*

MOST PROFITABLE BREED OF SHEEP.—A Canada West Farmer writing on this question to the *Genesee Farmer*, says; "As far as my experience goes, the most profitable sheep *are of no breed.* Buy poor and inferior ewes (of the native stock if possible), cross them with the best Leicester or Southdown rams, according to their roughness and other qualities, and they will pay from 50 to 100 per cent per annum, or more. This is simply taking advantage of the established maxim in breeding, that the first cross is the best. You thus obtain an increase in mutton of from 20 to 30 pounds, and an increase of wool of from 50 to 100 per cent., besides a great improvement in the quality of both."

CURE FOR WARTS AND CORNS.—The bark of a willow tree, burned to ashes, mixed with strong vinegar, and applied to the parts, will remove all corns or excrescences on any part of the body.

Horticultural and Pomological.

WILLIAM SUMMER, EDITOR.

WORK FOR THE MONTH.

South of this the work of gardening will commence at the close of this month, and *Peas, Cabbages, Onions, Radishes, Lettuce, Parsnips, Carrots, Turnips, Beets and Spinage*, may be sown for early crops.— Sow *Parsley*, and other *sweet herbs*. Plant a few *Irish Potatoes*, and, for an early crop, we have found no preparation better than cotton-seed in the trenches. Plant *Horse-Radish* and *Artichokes*, and do not forget to dress up and manure heavily your *Asparagus* beds, not forgetting to give a good admixture of salt. All the seed beds, and many young plants, will require protection during very cold weather.— Manure and prepare the ground for all Spring crops. Continue the work as for last month. Prick out *Cauliflower* plants in a bed under a north fence, and provide for protecting them from frost, when needful. If hot-beds are needed, as they will be for *Egg plants, Tomatoes* and *Peppers*, prepare them as follows: Mark off the ground six inches each way larger than the frame, on which the sash is to rest.— Throw out the earth to the depth of three inches at the bank, and nine at the front of the intended bed. The bed must be formed of fresh dung from the horse stable, or cotton-seed. Whatever material is used, must be of a proper degree of dampness to heat well —not *wet*, nor yet dry. With a little attention, a hot bed will be of great service in bringing forward early plants, and will well repay for the trouble of preparing it.

SUSANNAH APPLE.

This beautiful South Carolina Seedling Apple, which received the premium, as the "best late keeping variety," at the recent State Fair, is decidedly an acquisition to our already extensive list of Southern Seedlings. It was produced in the vicinity of Pomaria. Its merit is established, from the fact that it triumphed over *twenty-one varieties* of choice well-known Southern seedlings. The tree is a vigorous grower. Symmetrical, with a healthy, upright habit; fruit, large; form, oblong oval; color, greenish-yellow; stems short and stout, cavity shallow, calyx closed; flesh, yellow, tender, crisp, with a rich vinous flavor, highly aromatic. Ripens here from January to April. This fruit bore, for the first time, in 1858, and again produced a fine crop the present season, giving promise of being a regular bearer. The entire stock will be propagated next season, at Pomaria, and it will be disseminated in 1861.

GRAPES FOR FLORIDA.

There is no reason why Florida should not be furnished with the best table grapes in the world. It is the only portion of the South in which the foreign grapes will flourish, and the native kinds have been found adapted to many localities. St. Augustine is famous for the fine grapes grown in that ancient city. In Marion county, the Blands, a variety which seems, in our region, to be a meagre grower, has recovered its vitality and luxuriance, and, at Mr. REDDICK's, bore a splendid crop, the past season. The Scuppernong, at Gen. Scott's and Mr. Parson's, in the same county, produced large and luscious crops. Mr. Sommes, of West Florida, has published his successes with the vine, in that part of the State. Judge King, of Key West, informed a friend of our's of the most extraordinary production of a foreign vine, at that city—a production, the amount of which will startle the vignerons of the world, when it is published. We are promised all the data of this remarkable vine, and when received we will publish it, for the benefit of our Southern friends. In the mean time we would advise all our Southern neighbors to plant grape-vines. They will repay them in a few years by the rich, healthy, tempting, and luscious fruit they will afford; a fruit intended by nature for the refreshment of those who dwell in warm latitudes. There is no reason why Florida should not rival Italy in the production of grapes, oranges and figs.

A LARGE LENOIR GRAPE VINE.

Our neighbor, HENRY GALLMAN, Esq., near Pomaria, has, growing in his yard, a Lenoir grape-vine, which is not 20 years old, the measurements of which are as follows: It originally forked above the ground, but the collar has, within a year or two, been covered with earth. The two branches now measure respectively 29 and 25 inches in circumference, immediately above the surface, making together 54 inches, which gives a diameter of 18 inches.— This vine is closely pruned every season, and covers a diameter of 60 feet. It annually yields an immense crop of fruit, of the best quality. The original stock of this vine was sent to Pomaria by that eminent vigneron, NICHOLAS HERBEMONT, and being a believer in healthy stock, we propagate from it alone. The Lenoir grape is a native of South Carolina. The late Judge EVANS informed us that he had frequently seen the original vine growing on the plantation of Mr. LENOIR, of Sumter District. It is a seedling of the *Summer grape* (*Vitis Æstivalis*), and, as Mr. RAVENELL, in his admirable "Botanical Chapter on Grapes," in the November number of this journal, has stated, it has been disseminated under the various names of *Black July, Lincoln, Thurmond, Sumter and Devereaux.* We understand that it is now claimed that the Devereaux is a later ripening variety than the Lenoir. All these things show that there should be a verification of varieties of all the fruits of the South, and a standard name, authentically adopted, of all fruits cultivated.

TWO NEW PEARS.

No. 1. *Upper Crust.*—This fine early pear was produced at Pomaria in 1845. It ripens about the 15th of June, and here, upon its native soil, is *first-rate.* It is productive, bears early both on standard and quince; forms beautiful spreading pyramids.—It has delicate but very healthy wood, and, so far, has been free from blight. The Northern writers pronounce it *inferior,* but, to our certain knowledge, it has never been tasted North, but by Dr. BRINKLE, of Philadelphia, to whom we sent specimens in 1856, and who received them long after they were over-ripe. Under similar circumstances the Madeline, Bloodgood and Dearbourne Seedling would have been in similar bad condition. It ripens well on the tree, and assumes a yellow hue when fit to eat. It bears in enormous clusters, and, in the South, *is the very best early pear for table and market purposes.*

This was the Premium Pear of the State Agricultural Society, in 1856.

No. 2. *Dr. Bachman.*—This superb Summer pear first fruited with us in 1856, and again in 1858, the original tree produced over ten bushels. It is a singularly shaped obovate pear, of medium size, with a reddish russet tint, which becomes vivid in the sun. Stem long and slender, with an open calyx. Flavor rich, vinous and melting, with a remarkably thin skin; flesh tender, and as fine as a banana. The tree is of vigorous, upright, pyramidal habit, and grows finely, both on pear and quince stocks. It will undoubtedly make superb pyramids on the quince. We dedicated this pear to our friend, that great and good man, the Rev. Dr. BACHMAN, D. D., of Charleston, S. C. It was the Premium pear of the South Carolina State Agricultural Society, in 1858. We have propagated both these pears extensively in our Nursery, at Pomaria.

SPANISH CHESNUTS, MADEIRA NUTS, &C.

We have been impressed with the great value of Nut trees, and the propriety of planting, largely, every variety, in order to render us independent of foreign supplies of Walnuts, Filberts, Almonds and Spanish Chesnuts. We fruited the Spanish Maron Chesnut this season, and a tree not ten years old gave us a reasonable amount of fruit. It is a most symmetrical tree, and, for lawns, pleasure-grounds, avenues and road-sides, would, if cultivated, soon take the place of other ornamental shade-trees.—The Madeira Nut (*Juglous regia*) is a native of Per-

sia, (though frequently termed English Walnut,) and bears at an early age. An acre of this tree, in a dozen years, would produce a large revenue. It flourishes well in Florida, where its blooming would never be killed by frost. It is at home in South Carolina, and there are many large trees in Columbia, and other places in the State, which produce fine crops of fruit. The trees of Dr. EDWARD FISHER, Mrs. LYONS, and others, annually bear large crops of fine nuts. The Filbert would, also, do well in many localities in the South. Florida should grow the Almond extensively. Here we have frequently found it, and its yield is enormous. If we grew our own nuts, they would bear a large price, and would be more wholesome than the old rancid stock, which reaches our tables, from Europe. The Pecan-nut is, also, a valuable tree for cultivation, and usually bears early enough to induce young people to plant it. Our mountain friends, if they would devote their coves to the Butter-nut, (*Juglous cineria,*) could produce large quantities of fine nuts, for sale. It is next in delicacy to the Madeira-nut, and grows well in any spot of rich soil, amongst the rocks, on the mountain sides, and in the glens. Let us inaugurate 1860 with a trial of the valuable Nut-trees adapted to our localities.

Plant the road-sides with spreading Marons—they will give shade and fruit. Let the walnut have its corner in the orchard; cultivate and protect them, and coming generations of children will bless you, and—perhaps—crack nuts on your tombstones.

COUNTRY LIFE.

A charming title for an equally charming book, which has appeared, in beautiful style, from the publishing house of J. P. JEWETT, Boston. In the whole range of rural literature, America has heretofore produced no work at all comparable to Mr. COPELAND'S "Country Life," although practically adapted to the Northern latitudes, it is filled with thousands of applicable suggestions for our own regions. The details for the farm, the garden, the greenhouse, the grapery, are particularly instructive to amateurs and gentlemen of taste, who wish to improve and beautify residences, *farmeries,* orchards and pleasure-grounds. We have a class of men rapidly springing up, in the vicinity of all our cities, towns and villages—men who, snatching leisure from business hours, devote some time to the pleasurable avocation of improving and adorning rural homesteads—those havens of rest which all sigh for, as a place of comfort for the repose for the few last years of an industrious life of business. Our professional men, too, are acquiring a fondness for this kind of recreation; and the orchard, the vineyard, and the fish-pond, are now rural institutions, which come in as pleasing and useful adjuncts to the kitchen and flower garden. A lawyer or doctor, usually knows as little about rural improvement, as a merchant or schoolmaster. To all these, Mr. COPELAND's beautiful and comprehensive rendering of "Country Life" should become a text-book. It does as much for rural improvement and landscape gardening, as can be effected by any book. It has germs of practical teaching, which, if studied, will reveal beauties whenever contemplated with a view to improvement in the great art of protecting and embellishing Nature. We have long needed such works. DOWNING's books were well-timed, and awakened the interest in rural improvement, which must now take shape and form from the practical details of such authors as Mr. COPELAND. In all things complete, a text book, reliable and faultlessly concise and plain, we take pleasure in endorsing its claims to the attention of all who need a rural Guide.

For the Farmer and Planter.

MR. EDITOR:—Will some of the contributors to the *Farmer and Planter* inform us, if the killing of pork, on the decrease of the moon, will cause it to shrink? I was told by a Dutchman, several years ago, that there was a great difference in meat killed on the increase and decrease of the moon. I have learned, from experience, that hogs do better, spayed and castrated on the decrease. If there is any phylosophy for the above, please let us have it.

Log Creek.   L. S. J.

[Will some of our subscribers give L. S. J. the information he calls for?]

For the Farmer and Planter.

WHO BIT ME!

"I," said Mr. Pike. Yes, the Tree-Pedlar got me, and many more. He came in with his colored fruits, his show-pictures, and his specimens in magnifying jars, and I gave him an order. This order was made out, in the shape of *an obligation to take the trees and pay him his prices*, which prices were not stated, but made out when he came. My account stood thus:

12 Peaches,	$4 80
3 Cherries,	3 00
2 Plums,	2 00
1 Concord Grape,	2 00
2 Currants,	1 00
2 Gooseberries,	1 00
3 doz. Strawberries,	3 00
	$16 80

I have since found out that you, Mr. Editor, or any other Southern Nurseryman, would have sold me peach-trees at 25 cents; plums and cherries at 50; Concord grapes at $1; and strawberries at $2 per hundred, instead of $1 a dozen; and that currants and *gooseberries* won't flourish for Southern *ganders*. In looking over your new Catalogue, I find

that I could have gotten everything worth planting from you *for less than half of the amount* I paid to Mr. Pike.

If you will just publish the above, it will ease my conscience, and I will promise never, hereafter, to trade north of "Harper's Ferry."

"NOAH."

For the Farmer and Planter.

THE APPLE-TREE BORER.

MR. EDITOR:—I enclose a slip from the *Country Gentleman*, upon the ravages of the apple-tree borer. Of all the pests of the orchard, there is not one so destructive and so indomitable. At the very moment your tree begins to bear fruit, and you are enjoying the promise of a glorious harvest, you will see signs of decay—the leaves begin to change their color; the fruit begins to ripen prematurely; you examine the trunk, and find all right; but cut into the section near the ground, and you will find the rascal has gone to the heart, and your tree is dead. It is needless to talk about potash, soda, aloes, soapsuds, washes, or salt and ashes, or lime; we've tried them all, and they won't do. The fellow, when pushed, will bore somewhere on the limbs, in the fork, on the trunk, or in the root. We would like to hear of relief from some quarter, before we are decimated out of our orchard.

MALUS.

EDS. CO. GENT.—Why will not some State or County Society offer a premium for some short and sure way to rid the world of this (the apple-tree borer) pestilence? To-day I found four of these thieves in one of my young trees. They had entered below the surface of the soil, and worked their way upward a few inches, and there had snugly stowed themselves away for winter quarters.— They were mistaken; I cut them out with a knife, and killed them. The color of the leaves differing a shade or two from the others, betrayed them in their hiding places, and they had to die. Why don't our orchard books say more about these beasts of prey? Opening one of them in a highly excited state of mind, to-day, for a little consolation, I found the astonishing information, that the borer has been found in only one or two orchards in western New York, and they were all old and neglected! While the truth is, thousands and tens of thousands of trees, in this part of the State, are killed every year by the ravages of this enemy.— Who cares for premiums on fast horses, or fossil Durhams that are too old or ugly to die, while fruit trees are cut off, and fruit enough destroyed to fill their skins with dollars. Who will be the first to give a premium to the man who will slay the borer?

Canandaigua.   G. W. G.

BAKERS' GINGER CAKES.—1 pint molasses; ½ lb butter; 2 eggs; 2 tablespoonsful ginger; 1½ tablespoonful saleratus; 1 teacup buttermilk; flour to stiffen. Roll thin and cut in small cakes.—*Rural N. Yorker.*

From Harry's Magazine of Horticulture.

MANAGEMENT OF LAWNS.

No feature of a country residence is more important than a good lawn. Without this, a rural home is sadly deficient, however numerous and costly its other decorations may be. A fine house, rows of thrifty trees, flower-beds and vases and statues are all very well, but the eye does not feel satisfied unless these embellishments rest upon a broad base of smooth turf. Flower borders are desirable in their place, but if one's grounds are filled up with them it is difficult to keep them in a state of neatness; and even if kept in the best condition, the eye sooner tires of their daily view than of a simple, quiet lawn. The prevailing expression of the grounds of a country home should be that of *repose*, and that expression is interfered with, if the grounds are devoted largely to flower-beds. The flowers themselves are gay and exhilarating, and the sight of extensive parterres suggests the thought of the time and labor necessary to keep them in good order.

Not the least argument for lawns is the permanence of their beauty. In Spring the grass shoots up almost as soon as the snow-drop and crocus appear; and if the soil has been well prepared, the lawn in midsummer is almost as in the Spring; the fragrance of its frequent mowings is more delicious than the "extracts" of Parisian perfumers; the sight of children playing on the velvet turf, or of the shadows of graceful trees stretching across it, is worthy of a painter. The winds which despoil trees and flowers of their beauty, and the frosts which blight them, leave the grass unharmed. And in Autumn, amid falling leaves and prevailing gloom, it retains its cheerful verdure, until hidden by the Winter snows.

There is an air of refinement in a well-kept lawn. It distinguishes a place at once from the uncultivated wilderness of nature—it speaks of the land of taste which has fenced in this nook from the common earth, smoothing down its roughness, heightening its native beauty, and still watching over it with affectionate care. It links the spot by association with the elegant and happy homes of other lands and other times.

If, then, there is so much interest attached to lawns, it is important that they be well made, and afterward well cared for. A good lawn is a work of art—it does not come by accident. In some cases the first work to be done in making it is draining. This will certainly be needful, if there are any wet springy spots in the ground, or if the subsoil is cold and stiff, and retentive of moisture. The finer grasses will not thrive in a wet soil, but mosses and sorrel will usurp their place. The trees, shrubs, and plants set out upon it will lead a miserable existence, if they do not die outright. And draining should be followed by a thorough breaking up of the subsoil—be work to be done with a plow if the space is large, with a spade if small.

The principal reason why most lawns turn brown in Summer is that the grass has only a thin surface soil in which to extend its roots; and, as soon as that becomes dry, the leaves must of necessity wither. Trench that soil, and the grass will send down its roots below the reach of drouth, and will flourish in perpetual green. Manuring should go along with trenching. It is not enough to enrich the surface, for, though that may cause the grass to start well in the Spring, it will not insure its freshness throughout the Summer. If manure is incorporated finely with the whole body of the soil, it will improve its mechanical texture, and furnish food to the grass and whatever else is planted in it.

The importance of this thorough preparation of the soil can hardly be over-estimated. Too often it is entirely neglected. Most persons, in constructing rural homes, expend their means on grand houses, outbuildings, fences, equipage, furniture, and the like—leaving the work of preparing their ground for horticultural operations for the last thing; it is then done in a hurry, and of course imperfectly. Trees are planted, but do not grow vigorously; grass seed is sown but it comes up only in patches, and turns brown in Summer. As the proprietor afterwards walks through his grounds, amid his parched and barren grass plots and his dying trees, he exclaims, bitterly, "And this is rural life! this the Arcadia of which I dreamed! The whole thing is a nuisance!" We repeat it, then, that this thorough foundation-work is of the greatest importance. He who does it well, need seldom sigh for the "weeping skies" of England to keep his grass verdant.

The ground being well broken up and enriched, it should then be raked smoothly, and the roots of all weeds exterminated. If the space is large, it should be sown with grass seed. Red top and white clover make an excellent turf—two quarts of the latter seed to a bushel of the former. Some persons prefer blue grass to red top, thinking that it makes a finer and closer turf, and withstands drought better. It improves either mixture to add a small proportion of "sweet scented grass," for the sake of its fragrance when mown. Sow liberally, at the rate of three bushels to the acre, choosing a still day for the purpose, and raking lightly afterwards. A roller passed over the ground completes the operation. If the space is small it may be covered at once with sods cut from the roadside or common. Care should be taken, however, to select turf free from weeds and coarse grasses. Stretch a line across it, and with a sharp spade cut the sods into strips a foot wide, roll them up in balls, and carry them to the spot where they are to be used. Then begin on one side of the lawn to unroll them, matching the edges neatly, as a lady does her carpet, until the surface is entirely covered. Go over the whole with a turf-beater or an iron roller, and the work is done.

But a lawn once made will not take care of itself. It should be mowed once a fortnight, and when it borders on walks, carriage roads, or flower-beds, it should be kept neatly clipped with garden shears.— For mowing small surfaces, nothing is better than the English lawn scythe, which cuts closer and smoother than the common narrow field scythe.— For larger grounds, it is advisable to use a lawn-mowing machine, which does the work better than it can be done by hand, and much more expeditiously. A roller should be passed over the sward after every mowing. Once in two years a lawn should receive a light dressing of old manure or guano; and every third or fourth year, a little fresh grass seed should be scattered over it, to supply the place of any roots which may have perished.

Our lawn proper is now made; but we wish to say a few words about the arrangement of trees, shrubs, and plants upon it. In determining the proper position of trees, it has been recommended, by high authority, to throw a bushel of potatoes into the air, at random, and then to set trees wherever the potatoes drop. This advice was given to enable young planters to avoid the formality of straight rows and equal distances. But there is no need of such child's play. Simply to plant without any design or meaning whatever will not make a scene natural and graceful. Every tree should be set with a definite purpose, and all may be so arranged as to seem at home just where they stand. No universal rule can be laid down for the arrangement of grounds—each place demands its own treatment—yet there are certain general principles which should always be observed.

Obviously, the outskirts of a lawn should be so planted as to hide disagreeable objects. Why should your eyes, and those of your visitors, be daily pained with looking upon the rear premises of your slovenly neighbor, or upon your own barns and outhouses? A few trees, skilfully disposed, would conceal them. Why should your division-fences be thrust continually upon the sight? They suggest limitation and restraint; they perpetually remind one of the comparative pettiness of the beautiful scene around him.—Hedges and clumps of trees, set in flowing lines near the margin of the premises, would keep such fences out of sight. The more largely these screens are composed of evergreens, the better. In planting the boundaries, the largest trees should be set near the fence, and smaller trees and shrubs running out and dispersed over the ground within.

It is sometimes objected to this manner of planting the outskirts of one's grounds, that it is unneighborly and exclusive. "Leave your grounds open on every side," it is claimed, "to the inspection of the public; let every passer-by see and enjoy all that you possess." But must we not, also, throw open our houses to gratify the public curiosity?—We beg to know whether a man may not give at least a portion of his grounds so much privacy that his family can resort to them frequently without being gazed at by every street-goer? Is not a lawn more home-like, if it is partially screened from the dust and publicity of the highway? Besides, to say nothing about the need of protection from cold winds, there are few residences so complete in all their appointments that their effect is not enhanced by a partial concealment, the imagination always conceiving something better of what the eye is not permitted to behold. These things being said, it should also be considered that the proprietor of a pleasant country place owes something to the public. There are many persons of fine rural tastes who yet have not the means of gratifying them in lawns, trees, and flowers of their own; let them have a glimpse, from the roadside, of your beautiful grounds, and let the gate of your premises be always open at their call. The public taste generally will also be much improved by the daily view of well-kept grounds. And where is the man so selfish as not to find happiness in thus ministering to the happiness and the improvement of others? We hold, therefore, that, while one's premises should be belted with trees and shrubs sufficient for shelter and privacy, they should, also, be open at certain points to easy observation from without. Every visitor, too, fond of cultivated rural scenes, should be admitted to the grounds with a hearty welcome.

The position of trees on a lawn, and their number, will depend much upon the extent of the grounds.—In a large establishment, many large trees may be planted, both singly and in groups; but, in this country, most lawns are small, and large trees must be confined chiefly to the boundaries. In planting a lawn, the object is not to see how many trees it will conveniently hold, and then to set them out in rows, like an orchard. The beauty of a lawn consists chiefly in broad reaches of smooth, unbroken turf, surrounded by a waving border of pleasing foliage, with here and there a graceful tree casting its shadow across the velvet sod. As the lawn is generally a highly dressed scene near the house, the trees should be few, and those of the finer sorts, with neat bark and leaf. A few shrubs may find a place on the lawn. Those of good form and foliage may stand singly, as miniature trees; others may be set in masses. And here there will be room for the display of taste in the arrangement of colors. We have seen a fine effect produced by mingling the dark-green of the European Strawberry tree with the gray hue of the Missouri Silver-tree, and the purple of the Purple Berberry, the whole blended and softened by the lighter shade of other shrubs.

Our lawn will not be complete until it is enlivened, here and there, with flowering plants. We will not cut it up with large beds, and crowd them with straggling, ill-assorted specimens. Herbaceous perennials and annuals we will confine chiefly to a little flower-garden, kept by itself, on one side of the grounds, and mostly concealed from the lawn.—There, we will reserve a place for the old-fashioned plants, which our childhood so much loved—peonies, flower-de-luce, columbines, pinks, poppies, hollyhocks, morning-glory, cockscomb, larkspurs, sweet William—but there's no end. These, with their waxing-waning beauty, would not comport well with the highly finished character of the lawn. But we will cut out circular or other graceful figures in the turf near the walks, and fill them with plants of neat habit, and which flower throughout the summer.—Among these, we need hardly say, the best are verbenas, petunias, geraniums, lantanas, heliotropes, and perpetual roses. Several of these beds—those, especially, which border the most frequented walks—we will set with early-flowering bulbs, which can be taken up, or have their tops cut off, after their period of blooming is passed, to make room for the bedding plants. In this way, a succession of flowers can be had from early spring to late autumn.

A lawn, so made and planted, should be well cared for. Weeds should not be allowed to invade it; the grass should be kept short, and the flower-beds and walks always kept neat. Such a lawn will afford continual satisfaction.

SALT RISING BREAD.

Having seen a number of articles in the *Ohio Cultivator*, on the subject of salt rising bread, and one in particular, in which the writer, in her Letters from the Kitchen, manifests a decided preference for hop-yeast bread, I would like to compete with her before a committee of impartial judges, she using her hop-yeast, and I my salt-rising. If the flour is good and the rising attended to at the proper time, (that is as soon as light,) it will never become putrid. I will now give you my manner of proceeding with that kind of bread:

Early in the morning, say as soon as five o'clock, take a vessel of about a quart size, and fill it one-third full of water, milk-warm, adding three tablespoonsful of new milk, and of salt and sugar, each, as much as you can hold between the thumb and forefinger, and then stir in as much flour as will make a thick batter. Set it in a kettle of warm water, if the weather is cool, and keep it at an even temperature till fermentation takes place, which will be in four or five hours ; then take as much flour as will make two large loaves, and a teaspoonful of salt added. Scald about one-third of the flour, with water a little below the boiling point, (this makes the bread sweet and moist,) *the two main qualities in good bread*, then add enough milk and water to make the paste sufficiently cool, so as not to scald the rising, which will bear a pretty high temperature ; then mix in your rising and knead quick and thoroughly. Lay your loaves in good baking-pans, set in a warm place, cover with a clean cloth, and lay on the top of that a light pillow to keep the warmth from escaping. Your bread will be ready for the oven in about one hour. Bake till it is a light brown color and is thoroughly done.

Now, if L. L. will follow my directions (albeit she came from the direction that the wise men came from,) I will guaranty that her "Autocrat" will have no reason to complain of bad bread.—*Ohio Cultivator.*

CONCRETE FLOORS.

The lower floors of all the cellars of houses should be composed of a bed of concrete, about three inches thick. This would tend to render them dry, and more healthy, and at the same time prevent rats from burrowing under the walls from the outside, and coming up under the floors—the method pursued by these vermin where houses are erected on a sandy soil. This concrete should be made of washed gravel and hydraulic cement. Common mortar mixed with pounded brick and washed gravel, makes a concrete for floors nearly as good as that formed with hydraulic cement. Such floors become very hard, and are much cheaper than those of brick or flagstone.

REMARKS.—The foregoing is a good suggestion, as we know, from our own experience, that concrete makes the very best of cellar floors. But in cellars that are not liable to be flooded with water, there is no need of the extra expense of water lime or cement, as common lime mixed with coarse gravel, will do just as well. Such floors harden with time and use, and can be washed and kept nice, cool, and clean.

It is also a good and cheap way of flooring outsheds and back kitchens, when there is no occasion to hammer it in splitting wood or in any similar way ; it will last a long time and be found far superior to boards or plank, both in safety from fire and otherwise. We are using such floors, both in cellar and shed, and can recommend them from experience.

PROCESS OF MAKING.

Any farmer who chooses, can thus bottom his cellar of a rainy day, as follows :

Take 10 to 12 bushels of coarse sand and gravel to one of good lime, throw them in a pile upon the cellar bottom, throw on water enough to mix into a mortar, which mixing perform thoroughly with a hoe. Then spread equally over the cellar bottom, from three to four inches thick, and trowel it down as smooth and solid as possible, and in the absence of a trowel a hoe can be used to peform the whole

process. When well smoothed, leave it for a few days with windows open to dry, and the work is done. A cellar bottom to all intents and purposes as good as stone is secured for all time, and at a mere cash expense for the lime of perhaps 50 cents to $1. Who will not have a concrete floor in their cellar ?—*Wisconsin Farmer.*

KEEPING GRAPES.

I have admired the spirit of liberality manifested by the editor of the *Rural* in giving heed and reply to the numerous questions propounded, but have hoped the tax on his patience may benefit all around, as it makes the paper serviceable to all branches of a family.

1. I would be glad to have more definite instruction as to putting up Grapes for Winter. Where is the most suitable place to keep them ? I have been so unsuccessful, have thought I would not try again, but find others do keep them.

2. Is the Hubbard Squash used for boiling in Summer, or is it only a Winter variety?

3. Is the *To Kalon* grape as good (or nearly so) and desirable as the Diana ?   A SUBSCRIBER.

REMARKS.—1. Grapes for keeping should be selected carefully, taking only good bunches, and removing all bruised or unsound berries. Place them in a box—a layer composed of two or three thicknesses of paper, or cotton, between each layer of bunches. Put the boxes in a cool room where it will not freeze, though a slight frost will not injure them. This is the way we keep them.

2. The *Hubbard Squash* is a winter variety, and the very best.

3. The *To Kalon* is a good grape, not quite as sweet and rich as *Diana*, and ripening about the same time as the *Isabella*, perhaps a few days earlier. The fruit resembles the *Catawba* in form of berries and bunch, but is a little darker in color, though not much darker than we have seen the *Catawba* at Cincinnati.—*Ed. Rural New-Yorker.*

PLANTS—WHERE THEY ORIGINATED.—Wheat, although considered by some as a native of Sicily, originally came from the central table land of Thibet, where it yet exists as a grass, with small mealy seed. Rye exists wild in Siberia. Barley exists wild in the mountains of Himalay. Oats were brought from North America. Millet, one species is a native of India ; another of Egypt and Abyssinia. Maize (Indian corn) is of native growth in America. Rice was brought from South Africa, whence it was taken to India, and thence to Europe and America. Peas are of unknown origin. Vetches are natives of Germany. The Garden Bean is from the East Indies.—Buckwheat came originally from Siberia and Turkey. Cabbage grows wild in Sicily and Naples. The Poppy was brought from the East. The Sunflower from Peru. Hops came to perfection as a wild flower in Germany. Saffron came from Egypt. The Onion is also a native of Egypt. Horse-radish from South Europe. Tobacco is a native of Virginia, Tabago, and California. Another species has also been found wild in Asia. The grasses are mostly native plants, and so are the clover, except Lucerne, which is a native of Sicily. The Gourd is an Eastern plant. The Potato is a well-known native of Peru and Mexico. Coriander grows wild near the Mediterranean.—Anise was brought from the Grecian Archipelago.

HOW A CHICK IS HATCHED.

In conversation with Judge Butler, of Norwalk, a few days since, he explained the operation of the hatching process, which is so beautiful and philosophical, that, as we have never seen it explained in books, we repeat it to our readers.

The chick, within the egg, breathes through the shell; in the silky membrane-lining of the shell the blood circulates, and is thus brought in contact with the outer air.

The head of the chick is in a position as if it had been brought around under the wing and over on the back, a little one side, of course, in such a position that the least muscular exertion will press the beak against the shell, and about in the middle, and when any violent struggle is made, it will break a little hole in the shell. Now this little movement of the head, perhaps an eighth of an inch forward, turns the chick in the shell, so that, when the head is drawn back in its normal position, it is brought against another portion of the shell. The next struggle breaks a fresh hole, and so on, each struggle making a new opening in the shell.

These struggles, as the chick gains strength from breathing the fresh air, become more frequent. Finally in the course of half a day, perhaps, as it goes on turning itself in the shell, the little blood-vessels which originally formed a connection between the chick and the lining of the shell, are drawn so tight as to prevent circulation, or are twisted off; and, when holes have been punctured and the shell cracked about two-thirds around, the shell falls apart, and the young chanticleer steps into a new world.

Occasionally the lining membrane of the egg is so tough that the shell parts from it, and leaves it unbroken, except in the little holes described; and so, if not seen in time, the chick dies. A pair of scissors will effect a liberation.

It is dangerous to attempt to take a chick from the shell before it has, (as will be evinced by the cracked shell,) turned itself nearly, or quite, two-thirds round; otherwise the blood-vessels spoken of will be broken, and the chick either bleed to death, or be long in recovering.

The whole process may be watched, if the egg be kept warm in the hand, and observed as its struggles call attention to it. This will not interfere with reading or writing, and is instructive and interesting.—*Ex.*

CLEANING THE BARK OF FRUIT TREES.—The ordinary Sal Soda of the shops, when heated to redness in an iron vessel, parts with water and carbonic acid, becoming caustic soda, sometimes called "Bleacher's No. 1 Soda." One pound of this soda dissolved in one gallon of water, is the best tree wash in the world. Unlike potash, it does not kill or injure live plants, but rapidly decomposes dead bark, fungi, ova of insects, cocoons, scaly insects, &c. It may be applied with a sponge, and then suffered to dry on the bark; the first rain or heavy dew will remove it; running down the bark to the soil, where it is well worth all it costs as a manure. In bad cases, such as scaly insects, hide-bound trees, old trees with much dead or unsightly bark, it may require to be applied several times, and to be assisted by rubbing the tree while wet with a stiff brush and sand, or an old carpet or other woolen cloth, sanded. The smooth bark trees, plums, &c., become really polished by its use, and insects find it difficult to attach themselves. Old apple bark decays and is thrown off as it expands, leaving a new and clean surface, and sometimes producing fruit after having been useless for years. We believe that a clean surface to a tree is just as important as a clean skin is to an animal. The natural functions of the tree cannot be developed with an unhealthy bark. —*Working Farmer.*

A PLEA FOR THE CROW.—A series of articles on birds, in the *Atlantic Monthly*, understood to be from the pen of Wilson Flagg, of Beverley, Mass., has given that work a considerable reputation, in an ornithological point of view. In a recent number, the author speaks a good word for the crow, and we hope all our readers will read the following extract, and then judge as to the truth of the statement:

"He consumes, in the course of the year, vast quantities of grubs, worms and noxious vermin; he is a valuable scavenger, and clears the land of offensive masses of decaying animal substances; he hunts the grass fields, and pulls out and devours the underground caterpillars, wherever he perceives the signs of their operations, as evinced by the wilted stalks; he destroys mice, young rats, lizards and serpents; lastly, he is a volunteer sentinel about the farm, and drives the hawk from its enclosures, thus preventing greater mischief than that of which he is himself guilty. It is chiefly during seed time and harvest that the depredations of the crow are committed; during the remainder of the year we witness only his services, and so highly are these services appreciated by those who have written of birds, that I cannot name an ornithologist who does not plead in its behalf."

THE ELDER BUSH A PROTECTION FROM INSECTS.—We have seen it stated that an eminent English botanist made experiments in the year 1794, which led to the conviction that elder bushes would prove a protection from many of the insects which are so troublesome in gardens. If any one will notice, it will be found that worms, flies, bugs, or insects, never touch the elder. This simple fact led to experiments, and it was found that the leaves of the elder scattered over cabbages, cucumbers, squashes and other plants, subject to the ravages of insects, effectually shields them. And it is said that the plum, and other fruit may be saved from the ravages of insects, by placing upon the tree, branches of elder leaves. It is very little trouble to try the experiment, and we hope some of our readers will test this remedy and report upon it.—*Country Gentleman.*

HEN MANURE.—The excreta of birds of all kinds is valuable as manure, and if properly used, will invariably pay for the pains-taking. Lime, ashes or other alkalies, should never be mixed with hen manure: such treatment throws out the ammonia, and forms other compounds of lessened value. When dry muck, charcoal dust, woodsearth, or other cheap divisor, can be procured, compost hen manure with it, and if wetted with diluted sulphuric acid, so much the better; this will fix the ammonia as a sulphate, which is soluble, but not volatile, like the carbonate of ammonia. No farmer can afford to sell his hen manure to morocco dressers, even at four times the usual market price.—*Working Farmer.*

Domestic Economy, Recipes, &c.

SAVING CABBAGE.—The best way to preserve Cabbages green all winter, so that their good qualities shall in no manner deteriorate, is as follows :—As late in the fall as the weather will allow, *dig out* your cabbages that you have set apart for winter use, dig trenches, say 18 or 20 inches apart, and from 12 to 20 feet in length, as may be most convenient, and in accordance with the quantity to be preserved.—*Transplant* your cabbages as firmly in these trenches as they will stand together. When your bed is finished, raise a platform some 18 or 20 inches high, over them, which can be made of any refuse posts, rails, or boards about a place ; across this place a few bean poles or lath, and upon the whole throw a quantity of bean haulm, corn-stalks, straw, or any material of this kind, as a protection against wet and frost ; and you can eat green cabbage up to April, finer than if plucked from the garden in October.—*Germantown Telegraph.*

LABOR-SAVING SOAP.—To each pound of common hard soap, add from one-half to three-quarters of an ounce of common borax with one quart of water.—Put the water in any convenient vessel on the stove, add the borax, somewhat pulverized, and then put in the soap, cut up in thin pieces. Keep them hot, but not boiling, for two or three hours, or until the whole is well dissolved, and then set it aside to cool, when a solid mass will be formed. If the vessel is set upon a warm stone at night, the operation will be completed in the morning, though we think it better to stir the mass just before it is cooled. The night before washing, rub the clothes, where most soiled, with the soap, and soak in water till morning. The boiling and washing to be performed in the usual manner, but, it will be found, the labor of rubbing is diminished three-fourths. This preparation is adapted to all kinds of fabrics, colored or uncolored, including flannels, and is thought to increase their whiteness.

CLEAN MILKING.—It is sometimes forgotten that the last gill of milk drawn from the cow's udder is the best part of every milking. Careful reports made in England, show (according to a report lately published) that " the quantity of cream from the last drawn cup, from most cows, exceeds that of the first in the proportion of twelve to one." The difference in the quality also is considerable. Hence, a person who carelessly leaves but half a pint of milk undrawn, loses in reality about as much cream as would be afforded by six or eight pints at the beginning ; and loses, too, that part of the cream which gives the richness and high flavor to his butter.—*American Agriculturist.*

HOW TO STOP BLOOD.—Take the finest dust of tea, or the scrapings of the inside of tanned leather, and bind it close upon the wound, and blood will soon cease to flow. These articles are at all times accessible, and easy to be obtained. After the blood has ceased to flow, laudanum may be advantageously applied to the wound. Due regard to these instructions will save agitation of mind, and running for the surgeon, who would probably make no better prescription if present.

TO PRESERVE CRAB APPLES.—To 1 lb of Crab Apples, take 1 ℔ sugar ; put the sugar in a kettle with just enough water to keep it from burning ; let it boil up, then skim and put in the apples. Let them cook until you can run a straw through them, then skim out and boil the juice down to a jelly, then pour over the apples.—*Rural New Yorker.*

CHARLOTTE DE RUSSE.—Take 6 eggs to a pint of milk ; sugar to sweeten it ; strain into it an ounce of dissolved isinglass ; when baked let it cool. Make a whip and mix with the custard, cool it in forms. Lay in the bottom of the dish thin slices of sponge cake, alternately with jelly around the dish.—*Rural New Yorker.*

NICE CUSTARD.—Take the whites of 8 eggs, beat them to a froth, add 1 pint and a half of new milk ; three tablespoons of white sugar ; nutmeg to taste ; bake slow and not brown ; make a frosting of one egg and one teaspoonful of sugar, and when the custard is done, put on frosting and set in the oven 3 minutes.—*Rural N. Yorker.*

CREAM PIE.—Beat four eggs light and stir them into a quart of scalding cream ; add half a teaspoonful of salt, one teaspoonful of lemon extract, and two tablespoonfuls of white sugar. Line plates with pie crust, rolled thin, and set them in a quick oven ten minutes ; then nearly fill them with the cream, and bake half an hour.

REMEDY FOR FELON.—Take a pint of common soap and mix in air-slaked lime till it is of consistency of glaziers' putty. Make a leather thimble, and fill it with this composition, and insert the finger therein and change the composition once in twenty minutes, and the cure is certain.

CUCUMBER CATSUP.—To each dozen good-sized green cucumbers, add eight onions, all chopped very fine, and stir in a tablespoon of salt ; drain off all the moisture : put in pepper, mustard, &c., pretty strong ; place in a jar and fill up with good vinegar. *N. W. Farmer.*

A GOOD RECIPE.—To take out pitch, tar, resin, paint, &c., pour a little alcohol on the place, and let it soak in about half-an-hour. Then rub it gently, and you will find the alcohol has soaked out the glutinous quality, so that it will easily crumble out.

DELICIOUS CORN BREAD.—Boil a teacup of rice.—While scalding hot pour it on to little less than a quart of corn meal—4 eggs well beaten, a tablespoonful of lard, a teaspoonful of soda, a little salt, and enough sour milk to make a thin batter.

BAKED WHEAT PUDDING.—Beat well three eggs, add one teacup of sugar, two cups of sour cream, flour to make a stiff batter, one teaspoonful of saleratus, a little salt. Bake in a quick oven ; eat with sugar and cream.

OLD MAIDS' CAKE.—1½ pints buttermilk ; 2 teaspoonsful saleratus ; 4 large spoonsful molasses ; a little salt ; 2½ teacups each of flour and meal. Bake three-quarters of an hour.—*Rural N. Yorker.*